FATED

ICE WORLD WARRIORS : BOOK 6

JESSICA GRAYSON

ARIA WINTER

Purple Fall
Publishing

Published in the United States by Purple Fall Publishing. Purple Fall Publishing and the Purple Fall Publishing Logos are trademarks and/or registered trademarks of Purple Fall Publishing LLC.

Publisher's Cataloging-in-Publication data

Names: Grayson, Jessica, author. | Winter, Aria, author.

Title: Fated / Jessica Grayson and Aria Winter.

Series: Ice World Warriors

Description: Purple Fall Publishing, 2022.

Identifiers: ISBN 978-1-64253-513-6 (paperback) | 978-1-64253-038-4 (ebook)

Subjects: LCSH Space exploration--Fiction. | Human-alien encounters--Fiction. | Dragons--Fiction. | Shapeshifting--Fiction. | Science fiction. | Romance fiction. | BISAC FICTION / Science Fiction / Alien Contact | FICTION / Romance / Science Fiction | FICTION / Romance / Paranormal / Shifters | FICTION / Romance / Fantasy | FICTION / Fantasy / Dragons & Mythical Creatures

Classification: LCC PS3623 .I6675 F34 2022 | DDC 813.6--dc23

Cover Design by Maria Spada

PRINTED IN THE UNITED STATES OF AMERICA

DEDICATION

To my husband: You are not just my husband, you are my best friend and my rock. Thank you for all your love and support. I love you more than words can ever say.

-Jessica Grayson

CHAPTER 1

KYRA

A deafening explosion splits the air, startling me awake and rocking the ship to one side. Pain rips across my back as I slam against the bars of my cage. Terrified screams of my fellow slaves erupt throughout the cargo bay as another blast sounds along the hull, and the engines spin down with a high-pitched whine.

The doors slide open, and one of the Zovian Masters runs in. Light reflects off the chitinous, deep maroon shell that covers his entire body like armor, reminding me of a giant humanoid ant. His movements are frantic as he lifts two of his four arms to the cage bars. Each hand has a thumb and three fingers tipped with sharp, lethal claws. He fumbles with the latch a moment before it opens.

Another Zovian enters, quickly opening the other cages as well.

When he's finished, he tilts his ovoid head, and the two antennae on top move rapidly back and forth as he studies us. Frozen in place, my own terrified brown eyes reflect back from the multiple lenses of his own. His two large mandible-like pincers, where a mouth should be, click several times as he shouts out orders.

"Come, slaves! We must hide you before we are boarded!"

We scramble from our cages and quickly follow them down the hallway to the secret compartment they have hidden away in another hold. Every time they're boarded, they hide us for fear of being executed for trafficking slaves.

This isn't the first time we've been hidden like this. But it will be the last. I'm going to make sure of it.

They sold three people—in the cages across from mine—a few days ago. I can't help but wonder if all of us might already be free if we hadn't complied with the Master's demands that we remain quiet and hidden while the ship boarded at the last station.

The sound of metal grinding against metal echoes down the corridor.

"Hurry!" the captain calls out to his men. "Hide them! The Mosaurans are forcing the hatch!"

Mosaurans. My heart stutters and stops at that one word. I've never seen one before, but I've heard from the others that they are the good guys—executing any they find trafficking slaves.

For the first time in months, hope sparks in my chest. If the Mosaurans find us, we're saved.

"Get in there!" The harsh clicks of my Zovian master are panicked as he ushers everyone inside the secret hold. He seals the panel behind us as he steps inside and aims his blaster menacingly.

"Do not make a sound," he threatens. "Anyone who even whimpers will be killed instantly."

I have no doubt he will make good on his threat. But I'm

not afraid. As soon as the chance presents itself, I'm going to rush the Zovian and call out for help. I'd rather die free than live the rest of my life as a slave.

CHAPTER 2

RONIN

Narrowing my eyes, I stare out the viewscreen at the Zovian freighter. My image reflects back at me from the glass. My dark gray scales darken to match my dark-gray wings folded tightly to my back. My claws extend, and the muscles ripple beneath my scales as I struggle to suppress the urge to shift into my *draken* form.

The Zovians are hiding something, and I suspect it is slaves. Why else would they so vehemently refuse an inspection? "What are your orders, Commander?" my First Officer asks.

"Disable their engines and latch onto their airlock," I order. "We're going to board them. And if they are found to be trafficking slaves, we leave none of their crew alive."

It doesn't take long to disable their pitiful weapons and engines. From the amount of rust visible along the hull, I'm surprised their freighter is ever able to break atmosphere, much less manage to be space worthy.

As we latch on to their airlock, I make my way down the

corridor. Dressed from head to toe in my full battle armor, I allow my gaze to sweep over my warriors.

They are lined up in formation, battle-ready and eager to enforce the anti-slavery laws of our empire.

I tuck my wings close to my back and extend my claws in anticipation as we force open the hatch.

A sharp hiss of air escapes as it opens, and my eyes swim as the putrid scent of filth and blood fills my nostrils. They must have slaves aboard, nothing else could explain this horrible stench.

As soon as the door opens, we find the Zovian captain standing just inside. He clicks his mandible together in a frantic string of speech, trying to convince us he is a simple freighter captain and does not understand why we've boarded.

I rush forward and wrap my hand around his throat, slamming his back against the wall. "Your vessel is traveling through the sovereign space of the Mosauran Empire." My nostrils flare, and I narrow my eyes. "Where are they?"

"Who?" he barely manages as I tighten my hold on his neck.

"The slaves you are hiding."

"There are no slaves here," he denies. "I only recently purchased this vessel at the last station. Perhaps the previous owner had slaves, but we do not."

A low growl rumbles in my chest. His excuse is plausible, but I am not simply going to take him at his word. "Watch him," I tell my first officer. I turn to the others. "Search the ship. Leave no space unturned."

I stalk through the vessel, following the horrid stench to a cargo bay full of empty cages. I'm about to leave when another scent—something delicate, sweet almost—catches my attention. It is light, and I can barely detect it beneath the overwhelming smell of everything else... but it is there, nonetheless.

I follow it out into the hallway and toward another cargo hold. Several containers and boxes are scattered throughout, but the smell is stronger here for some odd reason. Something about this scent calls to me. As if it is familiar somehow. And yet that cannot be, for I have never smelled this before.

Closing my eyes, I draw in a deep breath and focus all my senses toward finding its source.

My eyes snap open, and I whip my head toward the far corner of the room. Two of my warriors enter, and I turn to them. "Have you found anything?"

They shake their heads.

I gesture to the corner. "Come. I believe something is there."

Together, we make our way toward it.

"Help us," a muffled voice cries out from behind the wall. "We're in here!"

Alarm bursts through me, and we rush toward the sound. "Do not worry," I call out. "We will get you out of there!"

I slam my fist against the metal wall repeatedly, trying to find a way in. It splits in two beneath the assault, and the panels slide open, revealing a hidden area with at least a dozen slaves.

Anger floods my system when I see one of the females locked in battle with her Zovian master. Red blood drips from her scalp as his clawed hand grips her dark brown hair tightly, jerking her toward him.

I rush him, but she's faster. A glimmer of metal flashes in the small female's hand, and she brings it down to bear. A sharp crack followed by a sickening squelch fills the room as the blade sinks deep in his thorax.

He releases an ear-piercing shriek and knocks her away,

sending her flying toward the back wall. She hits the metal panel with a sickening thud and crumples to the floor.

Rage blisters through me, and a thunderous roar rips from my throat as I rush toward the Zovian. He will pay with his life for daring to harm a female.

He throws up his arms, as if to shield himself from my attack, crying out in surprise as my dagger cuts through them like butter, separating two of his extremities from his body.

Dropping my blade, I place my hands on either side of his head. He will not be granted the mercy of a painless death. Gritting my teeth, I call upon all of my strength, pushing my hands together until his hard shell begins to crack and finally implodes, spewing green goo all over my arms and the rest of my body.

I wipe my hands on my uniform and tap the display of my wrist comm as I give the order. "They were trafficking slaves. Execute them all."

"Yes, Captain," my first officer's voice rings out.

I glance back at the warriors behind me and observe as they move to help the rest of the slaves.

My eyes turn to the brave female lying unconscious on the floor. I fall to my knees beside her and gently brush her dark brown, shoulder-length hair back from her face. The crimson trail of blood from her scalp to her face and the round shells of her ears tell me she is Terran.

We have only recently discovered their race after our crown prince rescued one of them from slavery and took her as his bondmate.

Her eyes are closed. My chest tightens in anguish until I see the rise and fall of hers, and I know that she is alive.

I scoop her into my arms and race for my ship. "Instruct the Healers to meet us at the airlock!" I yell to one of my officers.

He quickly bows and begins speaking into his comm, relaying my orders.

Cradling her smaller form to my chest, I rush through the airlock to find Healer Khiran already waiting. He runs his scanner over her body as I wait anxiously for his assessment.

"She is broken in many places and is losing her life blood internally, Commander," he says grimly. "We have to get her to the Med Repair Unit (MRU) immediately."

Together, we race down the hallway to the med bay. Carefully, I place her in the MRU. Her eyelids flutter and open; her dark brown eyes stare up into mine.

Ashaya. The word resonates deep in my soul, and my world shifts in an instant. She is my Ashaya—my Fated One.

She lifts a trembling hand out to me. "It's you," she whispers. "Am I dreaming?"

My heart clenches as I take her hand in mine. "You are not dreaming; you are awake. Her words suggest that she recognizes me, but I have never seen her before now. Perhaps she senses the bond between us, as I do. "You are safe now," I vow. "No one here will hurt you."

"Thank you," she barely manages before her eyes close and her head falls back as she goes unconscious once more.

"Khiran, help her!"

He pushes me back as he activates the MRU. The casing closes over her form and begins to scan.

Khiran frowns as he studies the display. "There are several partially healing fractures and internal bleeding. She is severely dehydrated and suffering from malnutrition..." His voice trails off as his expression hardens. He meets my eyes evenly. "The Zovians... you killed them all?"

I nod.

"Good."

"How long will she be in the MRU?"

"I am uncertain, Commander. She is Terran. We have

only recently discovered their kind. My medical knowledge of her species is limited."

With a slight clench of my jaw, I nod. I understand what he is saying. Less than a cycle ago, Prince Soran recently took Princess Liana—a Terran female—as his bondmate. She is his Ashaya—his Fated One as well.

Khiran places a hand on my shoulder. "She will recover, Commander. I am certain of it."

I turn my attention back to the Terran female. When I gaze at her through the glass, something primal unfurls from deep within. As the MRU works to heal and cleanse her, my eyes trace over her face. It is lovely and delicate with a smattering of tiny spots across the bridge of her nose and cheeks, only slightly darker than her golden skin. Her short, brown hair is spread out beneath her on the bed, and she appears so fragile my heart clenches.

"What is it?" Khiran asks.

I place my hand on the glass as if I could somehow touch her. "She is my Ashaya."

He inhales sharply. "You are sure?"

I've never been more certain of anything in my life. "Yes."

Staring at the Terran female, a deep ache burns in my chest. I have only just found her, and already, I've failed to protect her from harm. Taking in a shuddering breath, I close my eyes against the disturbing image of her crumpled form on the floor. I am not worthy of her.

"You should rest." Khiran places a hand on my shoulder. "I will watch over her until she awakens, Commander."

Fierce protectiveness fills me. The thought of leaving her side while she is still healing and unconscious is something I cannot bear. "I cannot leave her."

Khiran nods. "It is understandable."

Already, the pull I feel to her is so strong it is as if she is an extension of myself. A part of me that I did not realize was missing until now.

According to what I have heard of Terrans, her people do not have fated bonds like mine do. Not every bonded pair among my kind are fated. It is a rare and precious blessing from the Creator that many never receive.

"Commander," my first officer's voice calls out behind me. "Is it true that she is your Ashaya?"

I turn to face him. Still in mild shock at having discovered my Fated One, I was unaware of his presence in the room until now. His gaze is transfixed on the MRU and the Terran female inside. "Yes. I will need you to take command while I watch over her."

"Of course, Commander."

His eyes sweep to her once more, and it is easy to see the hope shining behind them. Ever since Prince Soran found his Terran Fated One, it has given many males hope. Especially now that Princess Liana carries their fledgling.

Terrans are the only species that are biologically compatible with ours. After the last plague that spread across our Empire, our males outnumber our females.

He crosses his arm over his chest and bows low before he turns and heads back down the hallway, leaving me alone with my Ashaya.

I rest my hand atop the glass casing of the MRU as I study her. I do not know the horrors she must have endured during her time as a slave, I only know that as long as I draw breath, I will be her blade and her shield.

The Creator brought us together, and I vow to be her weapon against any who would harm her. No one will ever touch her against her will again.

"Commander?"

My head snaps toward the med bay doors to find one of my officers standing in the hallway. "What is it?"

"There is some sort of anomaly showing up on our scanners. The First Officer sent me to ask you if you've ever encountered anything like this." He pauses. "It appears to be a wormhole, but it is not fixed. It is traveling… jumping locations somehow."

He holds up his tablet, highlighting the strange distortion on the screen.

I frown. "Whatever it is, it is unstable. We must navigate a course far from this anomaly."

I glance back at Khiran. It pains me to leave my Ashaya, but I need to assist on the bridge. Whatever this is could be dangerous for our ship to pass through, and I need to make sure our vessel is safe. "Will you stay with her?"

He dips his chin. "Yes, Commander."

I start down the hallway at a brisk pace, eager to fix this issue so I can return to my Fated One.

The ship jolts, and I stumble forward and grip the table, barely managing to remain upright. A high-pitched whine screams from the engines followed by a low groan of metal upon metal.

Red lights begin flashing along the corridor as alarms blare in warning.

"We are caught in a wormhole." My First Officer's voice comes over the speaker, full of panic. "We must evacuate the ship."

CHAPTER 3

KYRA

The piercing sound of sirens rings loudly in my ears and my eyes snap open to find a clear glasslike panel in front of my face. Reflective metal walls flash brightly in red as alarms continue to blare.

Oh God, I'm in some sort of container!

I turn my head, and the room starts to spin. My limbs feel heavy and numb, but I somehow manage to slam my palms against the glass; pushing with all my strength, but it doesn't budge.

My thoughts are shrouded in fog-like haze, and I think I've been drugged.

Desperation seeps into my soul. I have to break free of this box. My breath quickens and panic runs through me as I pound on the glass.

Across the room, the doors whoosh open, and a man runs toward me. My mouth drifts open as I recognize him immediately. I've seen him before in my dreams.

He's covered in smooth, dark gray scales with accents of

lavender that highlight the sharp ridges of his cheeks and brow. A small, bony ridge starts at the top of his forehead and spreads out across his skull in a V, disappearing into short-cropped, obsidian hair.

Large, reflective golden eyes with reptilian pupils stare down at me in concern as he places his scaled palm to the glass casing. Dark and lethal sharp claws tip his fingers and thumb. He is dressed in a black, form-fitting uniform that hides nothing of his heavily, muscular form beneath.

He is a predator in every sense of the word, but I'm not afraid. Something deep within tells me he's safe.

Then again... this could all simply be another dream.

Using the last of my strength, I raise a trembling arm to him, placing my palm against the glass, beneath his. "Get me out of here," I barely manage. "Please."

Another man—similar in appearance to him, but with obsidian scales—gestures frantically at me.

The first man waves him off before bracing his hands on either side of the casing. The thick corded muscles of his shoulders and arms strain beneath his scaled skin as he grits his teeth. A sharp hiss of air escapes as he pries the lid off and tosses it aside.

The alarms are so loud they're almost deafening.

He glances over his shoulder at the other man. "Get to the pods!" He turns his attention back to me. "We have to go. The ship is being pulled into a wormhole!"

Before I can respond, he lifts me into his arms and cradles me to his chest as we run out of the room and into a long metal corridor. I close my eyes as a wave of nausea threatens to overwhelm me from all the jostling motion in his arms.

I open my eyes again when I feel him move me away from his chest to set me down in a chair. A harness automatically wraps tight around my chest before he tugs at the straps to make certain they're secure.

The space in here is tight and appears to be made for only two people. It must be some sort of escape pod. At least, that's what I'm hoping.

"Are you all right?" His golden eyes search mine.

Unable to speak, I somehow manage to nod.

He straps into the chair next to me and presses a button on the display panel before him. "This is Commander Ronin. Can you confirm that everyone is off the ship and in the escape pods?"

I'm not sure who he is speaking to, but a moment later, a man answers, "Yes, Commander. All are safely away."

"It has been an honor, First Officer Lyran," my rescuer says.

"It has been an honor to serve with you, Commander Ronin," he replies. "This life or the next."

"This life or the next," Ronin repeats solemnly before shutting off the comm.

Without warning, Ronin slams his hand on the control panel and the escape pod jerks violently and ejects from the ship, pressing me back into my seat.

My stomach twists in a violet knot as the escape pod spins away. I try but fail to swallow against the bile rising in the back of my throat, and my stomach violently releases its contents.

My eyes roll up in the back of my head, and I fall away into darkness.

CHAPTER 4

RONIN

With a loud rush of air, the escape pod violently ejects, spinning away from the ship. I slam my hand down on the console, activating the engines to guide us clear of danger, but it's no use.

The vessel shudders as the engines struggle to fight against the wormhole's gravitational pull. Red lights flash in warning across the console a moment before everything shuts down, plunging us into darkness.

The agonized sound of groaning metal echoes through the cabin as we're pulled into the wormhole, and I worry the pod will break apart before we reach the other end.

A flash of light fills the viewscreen, piercing the darkness, and a gray-blue planet with silver clouds fills the display. I'm relieved that we made it through intact, but I have no idea where we are. Emergency power spins up, and I glance at the computer console, cursing in frustration as I study the read-out. This ice rock of a planet is the closest that can support life.

It's uninhabited. Not even named, it is only assigned an arbitrary number: ML-426. Its freezing temperatures and conditions are just barely suitable to support life.

I run a quick scan, and my heart stops when I detect a Mosauran distress signal.

It seems mine is not the only Mosauran vessel here. Dread fills me, however, when four new signals appear: V'lo-ryn, Aerilon, Lycaon, and A'kai. All of them set in a repeat cycle indicating a distress call.

I punch in a series of controls on the panel, trying to guide us toward the Mosauran signal. I want to land as close to my brethren as possible, rather than end up crashing in hostile territory.

The screen flashes red in error, refusing to respond to commands as we tumble toward the planet.

The hull groans as rough turbulence shakes the pod. A wall of flame flares brightly outside the viewscreen as we begin our descent into the upper atmosphere. Intense heat floods the cabin and panic twists deep in my gut. We're going to burn up before we even land.

I send a silent prayer to the Creator to keep our vessel intact.

When we break through the atmosphere, I stare in shock at the ice-and-snow covered landscape. Mountainous terrain and a sea of snow-capped trees spreads out before us.

I struggle to get the controls to respond as the ground races toward us, but it's no use. The hull scrapes the top of a snow-covered peak, and I squeeze my eyes shut, bracing for impact.

There's nothing else I can do. We'll either make it or we won't.

The pod quakes violently as we crash through the trees, rushing to the valley below. A deafening boom explodes throughout the cabin.

I pitch forward, and my vision goes dark.

CHAPTER 5

RONIN

My head is pounding as my mind slowly trickles back into awareness. With a low groan, I twist to look over at my Ashaya. My eyes go wide as I see her slumped-over form in the seat. The pungent odor of bile reaches my nostrils, and my eyes shift to the floor in front of her to where she seems to have expelled the contents of her stomach.

I rush toward her and cup her chin, tipping her face up to me. Her eyes are closed, and she is still unconscious. Quickly, I unbuckle her harness and scoop her into my arms. Her weight is so slight it is concerning.

Carefully, I lay her down on a clear space on the floor. My heart clenches at how fragile she appears. I retrieve the emergency bag and pull out the scanner, praying her injuries are not severe.

As I run it over her form, I study the read-out. Thankfully, it seems the MRU finished repairing her injuries before we had to evacuate the ship.

I inhale sharply as the display highlights a pattern of jagged, red scars across her back—each mark a branding from her previous owners. And from the look of it, she's had at least three.

Each scar is brutal and deep. If I could, I would kill every single person who ever hurt my Ashaya.

I pull the ion cleanser from the emergency bag and run it over her form, allowing the invisible particles to scrub all the dirt and grime away from her body and clothing, and even inside her mouth.

A small noise escapes her lips, and her lashes flutter open. My heart stutters and stops as warm brown eyes meet mine.

CHAPTER 6

KYRA

I open my eyes to find familiar golden ones staring down at me in concern. "Are you all right?"

Carefully, I sit up. The world spins for a moment before righting again. "I'm a little dizzy," I barely manage. "But it's starting to get better."

He holds out a metallic looking pouch. "Drink this."

"What is it?"

"Water."

I nod, and he flips open the top, and hands it to me. I take several sips and then pass it back to him.

"Are you sure you do not want more?" he asks, worry easily read in his features.

"I'm sure."

Already I'm starting to feel better. My mind isn't foggy like it was before.

"I am Ronin—Commander of the Kinshura of the Mosauran Empire and heir of House Lydoran. What is your name?"

"Kyra Martinez. Pilot in the Terran Space Program." I swallow hard as dark memories return. "Until I was taken, that is."

"Kyra Martinez," he repeats, committing it to memory.

Even though he is technically a stranger, I'm not afraid of him. He saved me. Just like in my dreams, there is a kindness behind his golden eyes. If he wanted to harm me, he had ample opportunity to do so while I was unconscious. My gut tells me he's a good guy, and I'm choosing to follow this instinct. "You can call me Kyra."

"And you may call me Ronin." His golden eyes study me intently. "How are you feeling now?"

I test my limbs a moment, surprised when I notice no pain. A smile crests my lips. How long has it been that I could move without some measure of discomfort? "Better."

I lift my gaze to the viewscreen, and stare in awe at the stark landscape before us. "Where are we?"

"Our ship was pulled into a wormhole. We had to evacuate to the pods. This was the nearest habitable planet."

"Habitable?" I ask incredulously as my gaze darts to the snow-covered terrain outside, wondering if the escape pod's computer may have been malfunctioning when it made this determination.

"Barely," he replies with a hint of a smile. "However, I notice several signals coming from the surface."

"What kind of signals?"

"Distress beacons. One of them was Mosauran."

"Was it from the other escape pods?"

"No. The signals were already transmitting as we were landing." He points to a band on his left wrist, tapping the screen with one sharp claw. A 3D image floats above it, showing a map of the terrain. He points to a blinking green dot. "We must reach this one. It is the origin of the Mosauran signal."

If I'm reading this right, I'm assuming we're the blinking orange dot that looks really far away from the green one. I cast a glance once more at the winter wonderland that surrounds us, and worry tightens my chest.

When I hesitate to respond, he meets my gaze evenly. "Neither I nor my people will harm you. My vow."

"It's not that," I reply quickly. "I'm not afraid of you, Ronin. I've heard from other slaves that your people—Mosaurans—are good." I look at the display again. "I'm just worried about our safety and how far away that location appears to be from here."

"Fear not." He straightens, puffing his chest out and tipping up his chin. "I am a warrior of Mosaura. I will protect you."

A smile tugs at my lips at his confidence. I'm glad at least one of us is sure we'll be able to cross this ice rock of a planet without issue. I've only been to Alaska once in my life, but this place reminds me a lot of that. My mind is already spinning with all the things that could possibly go wrong out here. Ice and snow can be very unforgiving, and I wonder what kinds of animals call this place home.

"We will have to avoid these areas." He points to the 3D image again and four red dots blinking on the map. "These are potentially hostile locations."

"What do you mean 'potentially hostile?'"

"I detected four other distress signals. Aerilon, V'loryn, Lycaon, and A'kai."

A shiver moves down my spine at the last one. I've heard of the A'kai before. All the other slaves were terrified of them. I've never seen one, but after all I heard, I hope that I never do.

"My people have a treaty with the Aerilon," he continues. "And an uneasy truce with the V'loryns. But the Lycaon and the A'kai are dangerous—enemies to the Empire."

I've seen an Aerilon before. They look like Fae, with drag-onfly-like wings. The V'loryns look like Elves with their sharply pointed ears. "What do the Lycaons and the A'kai look like?"

He taps on his wristband again, and an image appears of a man with golden skin, glowing orange eyes and pointed ears. I gasp as the picture morphs from a man to a wolf, but much larger than the kind found on Terra.

"They have a two-legged and a four-legged form," Ronin explains. "They are as savage as they are deadly, and they tend to hunt in packs."

"Hunt?" I ask, unable to hide the trepidation in my voice. "And those… *creatures* are here?"

He dips his chin in a firm nod. "But they are not the most dangerous."

My stomach twists in a knot of dread. If they're not the most dangerous, what is?

He taps the wristband again and the image of a man that looks like an Elf appears. He has green skin, short-black hair, glowing green eyes, pointed elf ears, and three slight cranial ridges.

"That's a V'loryn, isn't it?" I ask. "I was kept in a cage next to a V'loryn woman when I was with my first master. Her skin wasn't green though, it was tan."

"This is an A'kai." He points to the image. They look like the V'loryns, but they have green skin. It is believed they share a common ancestor. But the A'kai are evil. They are blood-drinkers."

He zooms in on the A'kai's face, and I notice two fangs peeking out from beneath his upper lip. I swallow hard. "Vampires," I whisper more to myself than to him.

I used to be terrified of vampires when I was a kid, until I learned they weren't real. Now that I know they are, I doubt

I'm ever going to sleep well again. At least, not until we reach Ronin's people, where it's safe.

He frowns. "What are vampires?"

"Monsters," I explain. "There are several ancient Terran myths about them, but my people... we thought they weren't real." I dart a glance at the A'kai image again. "But it seems we were wrong."

"We will avoid going anywhere near their territory," Ronin vows. He studies me with a piercing gaze. "You said something before you passed out. You indicated that you... somehow knew me."

I lower my gaze, unsure how to explain. But then I realize we're stranded together and alone. If we're going to be depending upon each other to survive, I need to tell him the truth. Drawing in a deep breath, I lift my eyes to his. "I have dreamed about you before."

He stills.

"I feel crazy telling him this, because it sounds unbelievable even to me. But I force myself to continue. "I... don't know why or how to explain it. But I know for sure it was you. It's happened so many times, I would recognize you anywhere."

He studies me with a piercing gaze. "I believe I know why this is."

I blink. "Why?"

"Because you are my Ashaya—my Fated One."

"*What?*"

"You are my fated mate, and I am yours," he says matter-of-factly.

My mouth drifts open. "What *exactly* does that mean?"

"I know this may sound strange to you." His brow furrows softly. "And I understand that your people—Terrans —do not normally have fated bonds, but—"

27

"How is it that you know so much about my race? Have you seen others like me?"

"My people have rescued many of yours. The Prince of our Empire found his Fated One among your kind—a Terran female that he rescued from the A'kai. She is his bondmate and Princess of our Empire now."

Hope flares. "What is her name?"

"Liana Garza."

She must have been taken after I was, because her name doesn't sound familiar.

He continues. "Our Empire has been searching for your kind to free them and offer them shelter with our people until we can locate your home world."

I blink at him in shock. "Why would your Empire do this?"

"Slavery is against our laws. But it is more than that." His eyes search mine. "Ashaya are sacred in my culture—as rare as they are precious: a blessing from the Creator. Already, the Princess carries their fledgling. Yours is the only other race that is biologically compatible with ours in this way.

"It is our hope that where one Fated bond can be found between our two races, perhaps there might be others as well." He pauses. "From what I have heard, Princess Liana of Terra dreamed of Prince Soran before they met, as well. Our Healers believe it may be how the bond manifests for your kind."

I've always been one to believe in destiny and fate. That there is someone out there destined for me. But never in a million years did I think he'd be an alien. Ronin has been kind to me, and I cannot deny that he *is* attractive, but we're still relative strangers. I'm not sure how to respond, wondering what he expects from me.

As if reading my mind, he leans in, his gaze holding mine as he speaks solemnly. "I know that we have only just met, but I want to reassure you. I give you my vow, as a warrior of Mosaura, that I will never force myself upon you in any way. I only wish to protect you. Will you allow this?"

My instincts tell me that I can trust him, and I stand by my initial assessment. Heaven knows I've been through so much these past few months since I first woke up in this hell. I believe that I dreamed about him for a reason, and I'm so tired of feeling alone in all of this. It's nice to have someone offer to watch my back. "Yes."

Something akin to hope flickers across his expression. He drops to one knee before me. "I vow to protect and defend you with my life, my Ashaya, until the Creator comes to take me from this world to the next."

He is too perfect. Part of me worries this is all a dream, and that I'll wake up in my cage again.

"What is wrong?" He cocks his head to the side to regard me.

I lower my gaze, ashamed of the tears that would come if I let them. I don't want to cry. I'm strong. I have to be. But it's been so long since I've had hope that I'm afraid. "What if this is all some sort of fever dream?" I whisper more to myself than to him. "I'm going to wake up, and you'll be gone."

His expression softens. "This is not a dream."

My fear makes me bold, and I reach out to touch his face. I have to know if this is real.

His scales are soft as silk beneath my fingers. "You're really here with me," I whisper. A tear slips down my cheek, but I quickly brush it away. "You're real."

"Yes." He places his hand over mine, on his cheek. "You are not dreaming. The Creator aligned our paths, Kyra. We are going to find my people and escape this ice world."

It can't be coincidence that fate led us to each other. Not with my dreams and this bond he claims we have. A faint smile curves my lips. "All right."

I love his confidence. When he stands, I note how much taller he is than me. The top of my head barely comes to his chin. My gaze drops to his heavily muscled body. The black uniform he wears doesn't hide anything of his muscular form beneath.

I glance out the viewscreen again. The sun hangs low on the horizon, stretching long shadows from the trees. If this place is anything like Terra, the nights will be much colder than the daytime. "I think we should wait to leave in the morning."

"I agree. We will remain here tonight. Tomorrow, we will travel toward the Mosauran signal and find a way off this rock."

It's as good a plan as any, I suppose.

My gaze drifts down to the med gown I'm wearing and then back out to the snow. "Are there any other clothes I could wear?" I gesture to my paper-thin dress. "I won't get very far in these without freezing to death."

His eyes widen. "Your kind can freeze to death?"

I frown. "Yours can't?"

He shakes his head. "We are able to regulate our body temperatures to withstand almost any climate." He steps back, and removes his shirt. "You can wear my uniform to keep warm."

Panic tightens my chest. My mind knows that he's not going to hurt me, but my body instinctively reacts with fear. Dark memories of all my times forced into the pleasure simulators flood my mind as he begins to undress.

CHAPTER 7

RONIN

I still as the acrid scent of her fear fills the cabin. "I will not harm you. My vow. I was merely going to give you my clothing. I do not need it to travel as you do."

Her eyes are wide as she draws in a shaking breath.

My heart clenches. I cannot imagine what she must have been through to react in this way. I wish only to reassure her. Carefully, I hand her my tunic.

She takes it from me, and slips it over her med gown. It's so long the hem hangs almost to her knees, the sleeves extend past her hands, and the neckline dips to one side, exposing a smooth expanse of bare skin across her shoulder.

"I'm sorry," she says, as the smell of her fear begins to dissipate. "I know you are only trying to help me."

"You have nothing to apologize for."

I decide against giving her my pants right now, worried it will only upset her further. Instead, I move to the other side of the cabin and search for an emergency blanket to keep her warm.

When I return, fierce possessiveness fills me as she stands there covered in my scent. I bite back a growl as I drape the blanket around her shoulders, desperately longing to wrap her up in my arms and wings.

Mine. The word flashes through my mind as instinct claws deep inside me. Everything within demands that I challenge her to the mating battle and claim her as my mate.

But I force myself to push these errant thoughts aside. She is Terran. I am not even sure that her people have mating battles. Even if they did, she may not wish to battle me.

She shivers slightly as cold air filters into the cabin from outside through a small tear in the hull. I wish the environmental controls still worked. I cannot bear to see her shivering. She said her species can freeze to death and my worries have now grown considerably concerning our expedition to find my people.

I cast my gaze out the viewscreen as darkness encroaches upon the land. It will only get colder in here and I worry for her this night.

If we are to spend the night in this pod, I must make it as comfortable and warm as possible. The primal instinct to create a nest for my Ashaya is strong. I know she has not chosen me as her mate, but it does not matter. I want only to care for her.

CHAPTER 8

KYRA

I watch as he uses the ion cleanser to clean the floor. I'm so embarrassed as he goes over the area where I threw up without so much as batting an eyelash. As he moves about the cabin, I can't help but notice his very muscular physique. Broad shoulders taper into a narrow waist. His entire body is thick corded muscle, and he moves with a grace that belies his larger form.

I notice him glancing at me discreetly out of the corner of his eyes. Although he is an alien, I cannot deny that he's attractive. We're so different; I wonder what he thinks of my appearance.

I think back on our conversation about the Terran woman married to their Prince. But then I remember that we're stranded on an ice world and the last thing I should be thinking about is how attractive my partner is.

We need to focus on survival. Everything else can wait.

He spreads two emergency blankets on the floor and then

offers me another packet of water and a nutrient bar. The bar is hard, so I place a few drops of water on it to soften it.

Ronin studies me intently. "Did the slavers file down your fangs and claws?"

"Terrans don't have fangs or claws."

His brows shoot up toward his hairline.

I frown. "I thought you said your princess was a Terran."

"Yes, but she was enslaved as well, when our prince found her. So were the other Terrans we have rescued. It is common for slavers to remove the natural defenses of their captives, and I assumed that is what had been done to your people."

His eyes are full of worry as they travel over me. Ronin's gaze drops to the nutrient bar. I hadn't meant to eat so much, but I was so hungry it's almost completely gone. "Do you want more?" He holds his bar out to me. "You can have mine."

"No, thank you." I smile at his thoughtfulness. "You eat it. I'm full."

A handsome grin curves his mouth, revealing two rows of sharp fangs.

"I never thanked you," I tell him.

His brow furrows. "For what?"

"Saving me. Twice." I pause. "Did you know when you saved me from the slave ship that I was your... *Ashira*?"

"Ashaya," he corrects. "No, I did not. It was not until I placed you in the MRU and you opened your eyes that I realized what you were to me."

"It's so strange, isn't it?" I frown. "How we could both be pulled to each other but in such different ways. Me with my dream and you, with this... bond."

"Tell me." His golden eyes study me. "In your dreams, what do we do?"

I lower my gaze, not wanting to admit it, but then

deciding it's best to be honest. "You comfort me when I'm scared or sad or... feeling alone. That's why I thought I was dreaming earlier. Because you're so perfect."

He blinks. "You think I am perfect?"

My cheeks heat in embarrassment and I stumble over my words. "Wh—what I meant to say was, I—" I swallow hard, completely flustered. "I just—"

"It's my scales, is it not?" He tips up his chin. "I condition them regularly. It is common knowledge that females cannot resist a male that buffs his scales to a fine sheen." He flexes a very impressive bicep. "Notice how they shine beneath the light. It is mesmerizing, is it not?"

I'm speechless as I stare at him, unsure how to respond.

A smirk twists his lips as he tries to suppress a grin, and I realize he's joking with me. "You're teasing me, aren't you?" I laugh softly.

He flashes a handsome smile. "Yes."

I laugh even more. After a moment I lift my hands to my face, marveling at the slightly dull ache of the muscles around my mouth. "It's been so long since I laughed, I almost forgot what it felt like."

His expression sobers. "You have been through much. I am sorry I did not find you sooner."

"It's not your fault. You saved me." A smile tilts my lips. "Besides, you've been pretty much how I dreamed. I'm glad that you're real."

Ronin takes my hand. "Now that I have found you, I vow that I will protect you with my life, Kyra."

Tears fill my eyes, but I blink them back as his words touch me. Deeply. "Thank you, Ronin."

While I appreciate him offering to keep me safe, I'm not helpless and I don't want him to think he's going to have to do everything for both of us. I had combat and survival training in the Terran Space program. I meet his gaze evenly. "And I will protect you as well."

His eyes search mine, and I wonder for a moment if this warrior of Mosaura—who is much larger and far more muscular than I am—is going to scoff or laugh at my declaration. Instead, he extends his arm out to me, and I take it.

He grips my forearm firmly as his intense gaze holds mine. "I will carry you, Kyra Martinez, to victory or to death. I will not leave you behind. We are bound to one another, and I offer you my warrior's vow, in this life and the next."

He speaks these words with solemn reverence. It is easy to see they are important to him... sacred. I meet his eyes evenly as I form my response. "I accept your vow, Ronin—warrior of Mosaura—and offer you mine in return."

He dips his chin in a firm nod. "And I accept yours as well."

CHAPTER 9

RONIN

When we're finished eating, we lie down side by side on the emergency blankets. I stare up at the ceiling as I think on our conversation. In her dreams, I comforted her and made her feel safe.

A smile tugs at my mouth. I am glad. I believe her dreams are the reason she is so comfortable around me now. And yet... as she shivers beside me, I also realize it is entirely unnecessary for her to be so cold.

I turn on my side to face her and lift my arm in invitation for her to rest against me for warmth. Her brown eyes meet mine in a questioning look. "Come," I tell her. "Let me keep you warm."

Indecision plays out across her features, and I half expect her to refuse. So I'm surprised when she rolls toward me and nestles into my chest. Cautiously, I wrap my arms and wings around her.

At first, she tenses, but then snuggles even closer. A soft sigh escapes her lips. "You're just like a heater."

She spreads her hands on my torso and tucks her feet between my calves. I'm shocked by how cold her skin is. "I wish I could say the same," I tease. "But you are like ice."

She laughs softly and then tips her head up to look at me. "I think we're going to get along just fine."

Happiness blooms in my chest, and I smile. "I agree."

I listen as the sounds of her breathing become soft and even. Despite my exhaustion, my mind refuses to rest. I cannot believe I have found my Ashaya. Finding one's fated mate is a blessing that every warrior wishes for, but so few ever actually receive.

While I am thankful the Creator has blessed me with this bond, I hate that Kyra had to suffer before our paths became aligned.

As a warrior of the Empire, I have freed many from slavery. I cannot imagine the horrors my Ashaya must have endured. Despite what she has suffered, it is easy to see the strength she carries within.

She may be smaller than a Mosauran female, but she is not weak. I think of her pledge to me. Kyra has the heart and mind of a warrior.

I lower my gaze to study her. Her face is relaxed in sleep as she rests securely in my arms. It seems I have already earned her trust. Now, I will endeavor to win her heart and prove myself worthy of holding it.

CHAPTER 10

KYRA

When morning comes, I'm completely wrapped up in Ronin's arms and wings. Carefully, I turn to face him and find him already awake. His golden eyes stare deep into mine, and my cheeks flush with warmth at the intensity of his gaze.

This is how my dreams used to be, only this is much better. He smells of ginger and spice and as I lie in his arms, I'm surprised that this doesn't feel awkward or uncomfortable.

I study his face, noting the sharp ridges of his cheeks and brow. The lavender colored scales there grow a bit darker as I stare at him, standing out in sharp contrast to the dark gray ones on the rest of his body. I wonder if it's his version of a blush.

"Is something wrong?" he asks.

Heat floods my face. "No, I—I was just admiring your lovely scales," I tease.

Ronin tips up his chin and puffs out his chest as if preening. "They are mesmerizing, are they not?"

"Of course, they are." I laugh. "I cannot stop staring at them."

"You may stare all you wish." A teasing smile curves his mouth. "I know you cannot help yourself."

I laugh even louder.

After a moment, his expression falls. "We should leave. The sun is beginning to rise and we must travel as far as we can before it sets."

"How long do you think it will take to find your people?"

"I am unsure." His gaze sweeps to the viewscreen and the blanket of white that covers the trees and landscape all around us. "This terrain is unfamiliar and we do not know what to expect. It could be many days travel."

I glance down at my legs. "I don't have any shoes. I—"

"You can wear my boots."

"Won't you need them?"

"No."

My mouth drifts open. I know he said he's able to adjust to the cold, but I'm still worried that he'll get frostbite on his feet. Before I can ask any further questions, he sits up, and I already miss the feel of his arms and wings around me.

Ronin packs as much as he can into the emergency bag. He offers me his pants to wear for warmth, and my jaw drops when I realize he is now completely unclothed. My eyes travel over his powerful, muscular form. From the hard planes of his abdomen and chest to the thick cords of muscle that wrap around his arms and legs.

My heart flutters as I take him in. He is pure, masculine perfection.

I'm surprised when I don't see the typical male anatomy below his waist. In fact, I don't see anything at all except for a vertical line across his scales in his groin area.

He said the Terran woman married to their prince is already carrying their child, but I don't see how that's possible if—

"Am I very different from a Terran male?"

My cheeks burn with embarrassment. "Not really." My voice comes out a squeak. "Just a slight difference. That's all."

He frowns. "How so?"

"Your—" I start, but stop, unsure how to delicately put this. Clearing my throat, I remind myself that I'm an adult and this is a simple statement about anatomy, and not anything to be embarrassed about. "You do not seem to have"—my gaze drops to the vertical line of scales on his groin—"male anatomy where males of my species would."

He follows the line of my gaze. "Ah. Your males protrude like V'loryns. Our *stavs* are concealed behind our mating pouch. When we are ready to mate, they extend from our body so that we may join with our partner."

He says this so nonchalantly. Heat scalds my face and ears as I force myself to nod.

Ronin cocks his head to one side. "Why are your cheeks darker now?"

As he studies me, my face heats even more, and I'm pretty sure my entire face is probably as red as a tomato at this point. I'm not sure I want to explain this to him, but I realize that we're going to be traveling together for a while, so we need to do our best to understand each other. "It happens when I'm anxious, or embarrassed or..." I swallow thickly before I force the words from my mouth. "When I find someone attractive."

He straightens, something akin to hope flaring behind his eyes. He flexes his biceps. "Attraction I can understand," he says, and I realize from the grin tugging at his lips that he's teasing me. "After all, I am a very impressive warrior."

I laugh.

"But embarrassment and anxiety... why?"

Without thinking, my gaze drops to his groin area again. Warmth creeps up my neck to my face and now I feel like I'm on fire.

His brow furrows slightly. "Is nudity not acceptable among your people?"

"Um... well, we don't really walk around naked, if that's what you're asking."

"Forgive me," he says quickly. "Nudity is common among my people. I did not realize—"

"It's all right," I reply, not wanting him to feel bad. After all, the only reason he's nude is because he gave me his clothes so I can stay warm. "You don't need to apologize."

Rather than continue our awkward conversation, he rifles through the emergency bag and pulls out a blaster. He hands it to me. "Are you familiar with this type of weapon?"

I study it a moment, familiarizing myself with the weight and feel of it in my palm. "I'm a decent aim, but I've never used one of these before."

He gives me a quick overview of the blaster, including how to adjust the settings for stun versus kill. When we're done, I tuck the weapon into my belt. It seems straightforward, and I feel better having something to defend myself with out here.

When he offers me his boots, they are much too large on my feet, but better than nothing. "These are really warm." I walk a few steps, testing them out. "Thank you."

I tighten the boots as best I can, but I worry about how I'm going to walk in these *and* keep my balance over rough terrain.

As if sensing my concern, Ronin adds, "You only need them to keep your feet warm. I will be flying us to our destination."

My head jerks back. "Flying?"

"Yes." He extends his dark gray wings out to his sides, and I marvel again at how beautiful they are.

"Won't you get tired carrying me?"

"You are smaller than my kind and weigh far less than a Mosauran female. When I held you before, your weight was negligible. My people are known for their strength." He flexes his heavily muscled arms for emphasis. "Trust me. It will not be a hardship to carry you, Kyra."

Heat flares across my cheeks as he twists in a different position while scrunching his abs to outline the impressive muscles that line his entire body. "All right," I somehow manage as my cheeks flush with heat. "I believe you."

I glance out the viewscreen at the ice and snow-covered terrain. "We just need to focus on survival," I murmur, more to myself than to him.

Ronin pulls an emergency blanket from our pack and settles it around my shoulders. It's so large, it's like wearing a robe, but it adds another layer of warmth on top of his borrowed clothing. Ronin uses the belt from his tunic to cinch it around my waist and studies me with an assessing gaze. "Can you move freely?"

I lift my arm and take a few experimental steps. I feel like a puffball, but at least I'm fairly warm in this and can move around without issue. "Yes."

When he opens the hatch, a cold gust of wind blows into the cabin, chilling me to the bone. Instinctively, I wrap my arms around my torso as I gaze out at the icy landscape.

This is going to be a long journey.

CHAPTER 11

KYRA

The trees remind me of the extinct sequoias back on earth but with pine like orange-red needles instead of green. Snow blankets the area all around us as flakes of snow twirl and dance on the breeze.

I glance back at Ronin, and his eyes are full of concern as I struggle to keep my teeth from chattering. He carefully cinches the emergency blanket tighter around me to guard against the cold. "Is that better?"

"Yes." I offer him a faint smile. My eyes travel over his completely nude form. He doesn't appear to be shivering, but it can't be comfortable for him to be without clothing in this blistering icy wind. "Are you sure you're not too cold?"

He tips his head to one side. "It is not entirely pleasant, but it is not anything that will bother me."

"That's good. At least one of us won't freeze to death."

Ronin's eyes flash with worry. He cups my chin, tipping my face up to his. "When you are on my back, you must press yourself close to my body to keep warm. Do you understand?"

I still can't believe he's going to carry me the entire way, and I feel bad. "Are you sure it will be comfortable for you if you carry me on your back? I mean… I can walk, you know."

"We will not be walking," he reminds me. "So you must either ride on my back or in my paw."

Paw? Before I can ask, he steps away. "Stand back a bit. I do not wish you to get hurt."

I take a few steps back. "Why?"

"Because I must change forms."

I start to ask what he means, but the words die in my throat as he transforms before my eyes in a swirl of snow.

I'm frozen in place as I stare gaping. An enormous, towering dragon covered in dark-gray iridescent scales stands before me. He lowers his massive horned head, and large golden reflective eyes meet mine. His long, tapered tail snakes toward me, and the tip wraps lightly around my ankle before falling away again.

Cautiously, I reach out and touch his snout, and he nuzzles against my palm. A puff of air escapes his nostrils, and a black curl of smoke tickles my hand.

A smile curves my lips as I run my fingers along the soft, smooth scales of his cheek, watching in wonder as the lavender markings deepen in color beneath my hands.

"You're amazing," I whisper.

He tips up his chin. *"And perfect,"* his voice sounds in my head.

My jaw drops. "I just heard you in my mind. How is that possible?"

"It is common for Fated bondmates to communicate with each other in this way when they are in draken form."

I'm not sure how I feel about him reading my thoughts, but I force myself to focus on the positives. He's an enormous dragon, so hopefully if we run across any hostiles, they'll think twice about messing with him. Even when he's in his two-legged form, he's impressively strong.

He puffs out his chest and a hint of a smile quirks his dragon mouth.

"You just heard all that, didn't you?"

"Yes." He full-on grins, baring two rows of sharp dragon fangs that would probably be scary on anyone else, but not on him, because I know he would never harm me. *"I agree with you. I am very impressive in both forms."*

"Don't get too full of yourself." I laugh.

He arches a brow. *"You are the one who said I was perfect."*

I roll my eyes in mock frustration. "Now, I've created a monster."

"A perfect monster," he teases.

He spreads his large wings and struts past me, and I laugh even louder at his joking. A puff of smoke curls out around his nostrils, and I realize it's his way of laughing in his dragon form.

Ronin's expression turns serious. *"As much as I enjoy laughing with you, we should be leaving, my Ashaya."* He lowers his head. *"Are you ready?"*

I touch his jaw, marveling again at the silken texture of his scales beneath my fingers. My thoughts turn to the bond and my dreams. This must be fate. It's only been two days and I already feel so close to him. It feels as though I've known him forever. Or maybe it's just that I've been through so much that I've decided to accept happiness as it comes, without question. "I'm glad that it's you."

He cocks his head to the side and I realize that I need to explain.

"If I had to be stranded with someone... I'm glad that it's with you, Ronin." I struggle to keep my voice even despite my emotions. "You make me feel safe, which is something I thought I would never feel again. And I know we've only just met, but... with you I don't feel so alone anymore."

He tilts his massive head into my palm and closes his eyes as if relishing my touch. When he opens them again, his gaze holds mine intently. *"You are not alone, Kyra. I am here. And I will stay with you always... for as long as you will have me."*

His words bring tears to my eyes, but I push them down. "'Always' is a long time." A faint smile curves my mouth as I tease him, trying to lighten the mood. "You might get tired of me before then, and regret your promise."

"Never," he states firmly. He extends his leg and looks at me expectantly. *"Are you ready, my Ashaya?"*

If anyone else called me "theirs" it would bother me. But every time he does it, I can't deny that it makes me feel warm inside because I know that he cares for me. "Yes."

I'm not sure why the thought of riding on his back makes me nervous, but it does. Maybe it's because he's so attractive or maybe it's a fear of sliding off and tumbling to my death.

"Definitely because I am attractive," he says, and a surprised laugh escapes me.

"Stop reading my every thought," I gently chastise.

His expression falls. *"Does it truly bother you? Because I am not sure how to stop. I... do not think all of your thoughts are coming through, but I am picking up several of them and—"*

"It's all right, Ronin." I rest a hand on his jaw. "I mean... it's kind of strange, but I'm sure I'll get used to it."

"Do your people not communicate in this way at all?"

I shake my head.

Even in this form, the way his powerful muscles flex and move beneath his scales makes me think of his two-legged form—pure masculine perfection.

His eyes widen slightly before he tips up his chin with pride.

I laugh heartily. "You just heard all that too, didn't you?"

His mouth pulls back at the edges in his best approximation of a dragon grin. *"I did."* He puffs his chest out. *"I am perfect. Just as you said."*

Another laugh escapes me. "*Now* you're just showing off."

His body shudders, and a wisp of smoke escapes his nostrils as he laughs.

As we joke back and forth, the muscles of my face start to ache again, but I don't mind. I haven't laughed this much in forever.

He cocks his head to the side. *"I can sense much of what you are thinking, but can you speak to me in your mind as well?"*

Softly biting my lower lip, I focus. *"Can you hear this?"* I project.

"Yes." His lips quirk up at the edges. *"Good. We will be able to communicate without issue while we fly."*

Carefully, I climb up his extended front leg.

A line of hard spikes runs along the length of his back. He snaps them flat against his scales so they can't hurt me, and I settle over his shoulders.

I glance at the ground. We're not even flying yet and I'm already worried about sliding off. "You'll make sure I don't fall, right?"

He turns his massive head toward me. *"I promise I will keep you safe, Kyra."*

My heart melts. When was the last time anyone looked out for me like this? "Thank you, Ronin."

I gasp as he unfolds his massive wings. Powerful muscles flex beneath me as they extend and then begin to flap, lifting us off the ground. Swirling snow and debris kick up from the sudden blast of wind, and I squeeze my eyes shut as the world falls away beneath us.

Cool air whips around my form, in sharp contrast to the comfortable warmth of his body as we soar above the tree line. With a sudden dip, he catches a current as we spiral even higher.

I gasp at the stark but beautiful landscape below, and my mouth drifts open in wonder. "This is amazing, Ronin."

I've always loved flying, but this is incredible. As we sail across the open sky, I've never felt so free or so alive. The mountains stretch out before us, their majestic peaks stretching up toward the gray clouds.

The soft light of the sun scatters brilliant colors of orange and yellow across the ice and snow, gilding the trees.

I gaze off in the distance, searching for any signs of civilization, but only wild and untamed nature surrounds us.

Strong winds claw at my form, threatening to rip me from Ronin's back. But I flatten myself against him and hold tight.

His body shakes as he fights the winds, struggling to align with another current. Tucking his wings, he slips into the stream, and the turbulent air grows calm again.

He glides effortlessly above the gray clouds amid the pale blue sky.

A wistful sigh escapes my lips. *"If we weren't stranded here, I'd think this place is beautiful."*

"Yes," he agrees. *"The landscape reminds me a bit of Mosaura —my home world."*

My curiosity is piqued. *"What's it like?"*

"A sea of trees such as this, but green instead of red-orange, cover the great mountains. Waterfalls spill down from overhead, cascading throughout our cities and homes. We build our structures into the obsidian stone walls. Our sun is orange, similar to this one, but our skies are lavender, and full of thick gray and white clouds."

The way he describes it is almost poetic. *"It sounds beautiful."*

"It is. If we find a way off of this world, I will take you there, if you wish."

I smile. *"I'd like that."* A thought occurs to me. *"Do you have any family?"*

"Yes," he says, and it is easy to read the sadness in his answer. *"My parents and my younger sister. I miss them very much. What about you? Do you have family?"*

"My parents and my two older brothers." Sadness tightens my chest. *"I hate that they have no idea what happened to me. They're probably so worried. I wish I could tell them I'm all right."*

He's silent for so long that I wonder if he even heard me. After a moment, he responds. *"When we escape this world, I vow that I will help you search for your home world and your family, Kyra."*

A tear escapes my lashes. *"Thank you."*

The sun hangs low on the horizon, stretching shadows from the trees. Snow falls steadily around us, blanketing the earth below in solid white. Ronin begins scanning for a place to shelter for the night.

"That looks promising," he says, as he flies toward a cliff face wall.

Several yawning cave mouths line the mountain. They will be a welcome haven from the cold winds and the snow.

Choosing the largest one, he carefully sets down on the ledge. We're so high up, I'm a bit worried about sliding off his back wrong and falling to my death.

He glances back at me, arching a questioning brow as he waits for me to dismount.

I make the mistake of looking over the edge to the valley far below. My pulse pounds in my ears. I struggle to make my limbs respond, but it's no use.

Sensing my fear, he wraps his tail around my waist and

gently lowers my feet to the ground. *"I would never allow you to fall,"* he speaks in my mind. *"You are safe, Kyra."*

He shifts back into two-legged form and then motions for me to wait here.

"I must check for any predators."

Fear skitters down my spine at the thought of some horrible and deadly monster possibly living in this cave, and I'm worried he could be hurt.

Ronin's head whips toward me, and he cups my chin, tipping my face up to his. "I can scent your fear, Kyra. But know this: I will not allow anything to harm you. Not as long as I draw breath."

"I'm more concerned about *you*, Ronin. I don't want you to go in there alone." I pull the blaster from my belt. "We'll go together."

A smile tilts his mouth. "I am a warrior of Mosaura. It is known far and wide that we are not easily killed."

I roll my eyes in mock frustration.

"And, I am perfect, remember?" he gently teases. "I will return to you soon."

Before I can reply, he turns and heads into the darkness at the back of the cave. He moves with a quiet and lethal grace that belies his larger form. I know he is strong, but I cannot help but worry that we'll encounter something even more formidable than him.

We know nothing about this world and the types of animals that make their homes here.

I hold my breath as he disappears into the darkness, straining to listen for any sounds, but hear nothing.

When he returns, a charming smile curls his lips. "It is safe. And, more importantly, it is warm."

"Warm?"

He nods. "There must be a warm spring flowing through these caverns. The back is very comfortable."

He motions for me to follow him, but I hesitate. He turns back to me, frowning. "There is nothing here but us. My vow."

"It's dark," I explain. "I can't see where I'm going."

He blinks several times. "Is your species unable to see in the dark?"

"We can see a little bit, but not much."

"Come." He holds his hand out to me. "I will guide you."

Without hesitation, I take his hand. The scales of his palm are soft and warm against my skin. He threads his fingers through mine and leads me through the darkness.

When we reach the back of the cave, it's still dark, but my eyes are slowly adjusting so I'm able to see a bit.

He's right. It's warm back here. Comfortable enough that I'm not worried we'll freeze to death during the night.

"I will make a nest for you," Ronin says, interrupting my thoughts.

"A... nest?"

"Yes. It is an old term," he explains. "My people used to make their homes in caves such as these. It was the job of the male to make a nest for the female and to guard and protect it."

"And now? What do you do for your homes?"

A smile quirks his lips. "We are not a primitive people if that is what you are asking. My home is quite comfortable back on Mosaura. I believe you will like it when I take you there."

I love how confident he is that we'll make it off this planet and how he's already planning a future that include me in it. I like knowing that if we make it off this planet, he won't just abandon me. Not that I thought he would, but it's comforting to be reassured.

"While my people continue to search for your home world, you can either travel with me on my ship or remain on Mosaura with my family." He pauses. "You did not have a chance to meet them, but I'm sure you will like my crew if you choose to stay on my vessel."

His optimism is contagious, and it makes me think of my own people and my crew. "You said that your Empire had already rescued several Terrans. Where do they live?"

"They have been given housing. A few of them have taken jobs as transport pilots, and some are working with our engineers, scientists, and healers."

He studies me a moment with something akin to guilt flashing behind his eyes. "I do not wish to pressure you into thinking you must stay with me, Kyra. I simply—"

"It's not that," I quickly reassure him. "I love that you want me to stay with you. I was just thinking about my crew… hoping that maybe some of them have already been rescued by your people."

His expression falls. "When you were taken, did you see any of the others?"

"No. We were in stasis sleep when we were abducted. When I woke up, I was alone in a cell. I hate not knowing what may have happened to them." I swallow against the lump in my throat. "All of us were close… like family."

"There is still hope," he offers. "My people and the Aerilon have been searching for yours. So many have been recovered. And we are actively searching for Terra to return them to their home world. We will find it. I am certain of this."

Knowing that his people and the Aerilon are searching for mine and for our home world makes me hopeful, but I can't help but worry for Ronin's crew as well. "Do you think any of your crew may have crashed here on this planet like we did?"

"If they did, I did not detect their signals."

He arranges the emergency blankets on the ground and then rifles through the pack to retrieve food and water. He gives me a nutrient bar for me and then offers me half of his as well.

"You eat it," I tell him.

Ronin shakes his head. "I would prefer you have it. You need to regain your strength."

I glance down my form, only now realizing how thin I am from the past few months of my captivity. The Masters often forgot to feed us.

But still, I don't want to take from him. "You need to keep up *your* strength," I insist. "*You* are the one doing all the flying, Ronin."

Instead of arguing like I expect, he simply dips his chin in a subtle nod and then eats the rest of the nutrient bar. He turns his gaze toward the cave entrance. "We have enough rations for a few days, but I will have to eventually hunt if we do not find my people within the week."

I hate the idea of him having to go off into this wilderness to look for food and hunt down who knows what kind of creatures that make their home on this harsh world.

When we're finished eating, he settles beside me beneath the blankets. Despite the fact that the cave is warmer than it is outside, it's still cold in here.

"Come." He lifts his arm. "I will keep you warm."

I know we slept together last night, but it's still awkward, especially since I'm attracted to him.

He's made it no secret that he wants me, but I'm afraid of just rushing into something. What we have right now is good, and I don't want to ruin it. I'm attracted to him and I'm comfortable with him, but there is still so much we don't know about each other.

I scoot toward Ronin, and he tugs me against him, wrapping me up in his strong arms and wings. His masculine scent of ginger and spice surrounds me.

When I lift my head, the warmth of his breath skates

across my skin. My heart pounds, and my gaze drops to his full, perfect lips. In my dreams, I never kissed him, but I always wanted to. Now that he's here and I know that he's real, I find myself wondering what it would be like to feel his mouth against mine.

Softly shaking my head, I push aside these errant thoughts. I need to understand more about this bond he says we have and what exactly he expects. I mean… for all I know, his species might not even be monogamous… or maybe they take harems. I'm not sure how I'd feel about that. I have so many questions, I'm not sure what to ask first.

CHAPTER 12

RONIN

I love that she does not hesitate to nestle into me. Fierce protectiveness fills me as I wrap my wings around her smaller form, holding her close to my chest.

I cannot help myself from softly nuzzling her hair. She smells of *ylori* flowers. I used to grow them on the balcony of my bedroom back on Mosaura. Flaring my nostrils, I drink in her scent.

Mine. The word moves through me.

As she lies against me, her entire body molded to my own, I long more than anything to claim her as my mate. Already, I can imagine taking her back with me to Mosaura. My family would be thrilled to know I've found my Ashaya. My mother, especially, has wished for me to take a mate and have fledglings.

Sighing heavily, I glance at Kyra. She may decide she does not want me as her mate. She has only recently been freed, and a relationship is probably the last thing on her mind. As much as I desire her, I know I must wait for her to decide how she feels. It is enough that she allows me to hold her like this. That she gives me such trust is humbling.

As the wind whistles outside the cave entrance, I understand that these are not pressing concerns. Survival is more important right now, but I cannot help but wonder about the future. If I want Kyra to choose me, I must prove myself to her. Show her that I am a worthy male to stand by her side. I—

"You said I'm your Ashaya," she begins, interrupting my thoughts. "But that not everyone finds their fated mate. So, how do you choose someone otherwise?"

"The *shav-rhokan*."

"What is that?"

"The mating battle."

She goes still. "What does that entail?"

"In my culture, if you are interested in taking someone as your mate, you challenge them to fight, to determine if they are a worthy mate."

"Umm… that sounds… different," she says, and I note the cautious tone of her voice.

"Mosauran females are larger than the males. If a male is interested in a female, he will wait until she goes into her mating heat. Once she does, he will go to her and present himself as a potential suitor.

"If she declares shav-rhokan, it means she accepts his challenge. They will then fight. If he is able to defeat her, he then gives her his mark as he joins his body to hers, and they become a mated pair."

What I do not tell her is that, even then, it is still a battle. Mosauran females are known for their aggression during their heat. Many males are injured during the first few matings. "How do your people choose a mate?"

"We spend time together. Talking about ourselves and getting to know each other better."

Hope sparks in my chest. "Similar to what we are doing now?"

"Um… yes."

This is good. This means she is already considering me as a potential mate. Already, I know that she finds me attractive. Now, I must prove myself a worthy mate so that she will choose me as hers.

CHAPTER 13

KYRA

The shav-rhokan sounds violent and intense—in complete contrast to how I view Ronin. He is so much stronger than me, but he is also so very gentle. He puts my needs and comfort above his own in all things. I have no doubt about where I stand with him. Through his actions and his words, I know that I'm his priority.

It's strange that we haven't known each other long, and yet it feels as if I've known him forever. Maybe it's because we're stranded on a world that is alien to us both. They teach us in the Terran Space Program about how shared survival can bond two people very quickly. Or maybe it's this bond we have between us.

As we spend more time talking about the differences between our two cultures, I'm struck by how easy the conversation flows. I feel comfortable with him, and more importantly, I already trust him.

When I shift slightly, he asks me if I'm warm enough or if

I would like more food or water. He's so caring and kind. I cannot remember the last time anyone cared for me like this.

I rest my palm on his chest, and my head on his shoulder as he keeps me warmly wrapped up in his strong arms and wings. It's been a long day and I'm so tired, it's hard to keep my eyes open.

Gently, Ronin nuzzles my hair. "Sleep, Kyra. I will keep watch for us both."

I somehow manage to nod and then close my eyes, drifting away into oblivion.

I wake a few times during the night and press my palm to his chest. I feel the familiar rhythm of his heart as it beats beneath my hand, and then trace my fingers lightly across his silken scales, reassuring myself that this is real. It isn't a dream. He is truly here, and I am safe.

A loud roar startles me awake, and my eyes snap open to pitch-black darkness. Fear spikes through me, but then I feel Ronin's arms and wings tighten around my form, and I remember where we are. "What was that?" I whisper.

"A predator," he says in a voice so low I almost miss it. "It is in the valley below. I believe it can scent our presence here."

Panic snakes down my spine. A sliver of moonlight spills into the cave from outside, affording me just enough illumination that I can barely make out Ronin's face. "Are we safe up here?"

His arms and wings loosen around me. "I must investigate this creature. See what it is that dares think it might hunt us."

He shifts as if to sit up, but I grip his arm. "Wait," I whisper urgently. "What if it attacks you?"

"I am a warrior of Mosaura," he replies, matter-of-factly, as if that should be enough to put my mind at ease.

"I know." I don't want to wound his pride, but I also do not want him to be overly confident in the face of potential danger. "But this creature might be bigger than you... deadlier and—"

"I doubt it would rival my draken form."

Men and their pride. "Just stay here. Please."

Ronin carefully untangles himself from my arms and stands. "Wait here. I will only be a moment."

I sit up, waving my arm out to find him, since I cannot see very well in the darkness, but I can already hear his footsteps retreating. A shadow of his outline is visible near the cavern entrance as he heads outside. "Ronin," I whisper urgently, afraid to make any more noise than I already am. "Wait!"

He hesitates a beat, but then continues walking. I watch in awe as he transforms into his draken form and then spreads his wings a moment before he drops off the ledge, disappearing from view.

I scramble to my feet and rush toward the cave mouth. I scan the darkness below and notice his shadow gliding out over the forest. As he flies further out, I lose sight of him completely. It's too dark for me to see anything else.

A deafening roar echoes through the forest, spiking fear in my heart. I go completely still as I search the skies for any sign of Ronin, holding my breath and praying that I'll hear him somehow.

I try to reach him with my mind. *"Ronin!"*

My pulse pounds in my ears as another roar sounds from below, followed by a chorus of others. A loud cry rises from the woods—the sound frantic and desperate. It's followed quickly by another bellowing roar that I hope is Ronin, but I can't be sure.

Despite the cold, a bead of sweat trickles down my spine

as I listen to the obvious sounds of fighting. I'm paralyzed with worry, so afraid that something has happened to him.

It was reckless of him to leave like he did. He could be dying down there, and I wouldn't even know. I can do nothing but wait. I feel useless as I stand at the cavern entrance, praying that he's all right.

I palm the blaster at my belt, but then realize the futility of this. I'm so far up the mountain, even if he called out, I'd be unable to reach him fast enough to make any difference. I curl my hands into fists at my sides to still their shaking. He gave me his warrior's vow that we would watch out for each other.

And yet, he left me, instead of taking me along for help. I may not be a dragon, but I know how to use a blaster.

"I am all right, Kyra," his voice sounds in my mind.

I only have a moment to be relieved before another roar echoes through the woods, followed by eerie silence.

A shadow glides into view, and I release the breath I hadn't realized I was holding when I recognize the shape as Ronin flies back to the cavern.

When he alights on the ledge beside me, he quickly transforms into his two-legged state. I'm so relieved he's back, I rush forward and stretch up on my toes, wrapping my arms around his neck as I hold him close.

Cautiously, he slips his arms around my waist in return.

"I was so worried," I whisper.

"I told you I was all right," he murmurs.

"Yes, but then I heard more fighting and I—" My voice catches, as emotions lodge in my throat. "You have to be careful, Ronin."

"A warrior's life is not without risk," he whispers.

Clenching my jaw, I bite back my anger. I don't want to lash out at him, but I hate that he went out there alone. I'm not useless.

With one arm behind my back, he slips the other up under my knees and hoists me to his chest. He gently nuzzles my hair as he carries me toward the back of the cave. "It is all right. I have killed the creatures that hunt us. You can sleep without worry, my Ashaya."

If being *his Ashaya* means that he is supposed to put himself in danger to shield me, I want to protest that I'm technically not his. Not yet, anyway. I want to remind him that we swore to protect each other. But I'm too wound up to argue, and I'm just so glad he's back and that he's safe.

He carefully lays me back down and then pulls me close against him. He folds his wings around me and whispers soothingly in my ear. "We are safe here, Kyra," he reassures me. "I will not let anything hurt you."

"But what about you?" I counter. "You could have been hurt."

"I am a warrior of Mosaura."

Anger simmers in my chest. "Yes, but you're not invincible. If you had been hurt or if you'd died, I would never have forgiven you."

A soft laugh escapes him. "I would hate to be dead and know that you didn't forgive me for it."

I narrow my eyes, but a smile tugs at my lips as I try but fail to hold onto my anger in the face of his teasing.

"Please, do not be upset with me." He cups my cheek. "They were predators and they had already caught your scent. I will allow nothing to draw breath that is a threat to you, and I will do anything to keep you safe, my Ashaya."

If there was any lingering doubt in my mind that he truly cares for me, it has been completely erased. As I nestle against him, I enjoy the feel of his strong body against mine as he keeps me securely wrapped up in his wings. Part of me still worries that this is all a dream, and none of it is real.

"We're supposed to be a team." I rest my hand on his

chest, feeling his strong heart beating beneath my palm, reassuring me that he is truly here. "We swore a warrior's vow to each other, Ronin."

"Forgive me," he murmurs. "It is instinct to protect you. I want only to shield you from any harm, Kyra."

"You can't protect against everything."

"I am a warrior of Mosaura." He tips up his chin. "I—"

"You are strong, and you are brave, and you are selfless." In the dark, I trace my hand up his arm to his face and cup his cheek.

"Do not forget 'perfect.'" I feel his grin beneath my palm.

"*And* perfect," I add, trying not to laugh because what I need to say is important. "You say that we're fated to each other. And we have this bond between us and I've dreamed of you before and—" I stop, unsure how to express what I want to say.

Drawing in a deep breath, I continue. "Even though we only recently met, I already feel close to you. I can't explain it, other than to say that this feels right. But if this is going to work between us, we *have* to be partners. Do you understand? You can't just run off to face danger and leave me behind, wondering if you're all right." I pause. "I am not helpless, Ronin. I've had training and I'm a decent aim. I want to be there for you, like you are for me."

"I understand," he replies solemnly. "Does this mean you have decided?"

"Decided what?"

"That you wish to take me as your mate."

This is literally day two of knowing each other. My heart is telling me to jump, but my mind is urging me to hold back. I must take too long to answer because he lowers his head.

"I will not pressure you. If you do not want me as yours, I will accept it, Kyra. And I know that I am probably very different from a Terran male. I will understand if you do not want me. I only wish to protect you."

A smile tugs at my lips at his sincere and touching words. "I believe that honesty should be the foundation for a relationship. Don't you agree?"

He nods beneath my hand.

"So, I will be completely honest with you now."

He stills, and even though I cannot see him clearly in the darkness, I can feel his gaze heavy upon me as he waits with bated breath for me to speak.

"I am attracted to you, and you are everything I could possibly look for in a partner. Everything you have done from the moment we met is to put my needs and comforts above your own. I know exactly where I stand with you. You make me feel as though I am the most important thing in the world to you."

"You are," he insists. "You are everything."

"But how do you know that you truly want *me*, Ronin? How do you know it's not just the bond that makes you feel this way?"

"I do not understand."

"For you, this is it. The bond is an absolute. But for me... my kind do not have fated bonds. This is all new. My people... we get to know each other before we decide if we're going to be with someone for forever. And while this feels right... I want to make sure that it is. I want to know you better and for you to know me before we just jump into this relationship wholeheartedly." I pause. "Do you understand?"

"I do," he says solemnly. "What would you like to know about me? Present your list of questions and I will answer them all this night."

A smile crests my lips at his eagerness. "It's not just about questions, Ronin."

He tips his head to the side. "What do you mean?"

"It's also about learning how you react and respond to situations and how we are around each other. I mean… What if I snore and it drives you crazy? Some guys really hate that, you know."

"You *do* snore," he replies, and my jaw drops. "And it is adorable."

"I *do not* snore," I deny vehemently.

"I thought you wished for honesty."

"I do, I just—"

"And you drooled a bit in your sleep last night as well," he adds. "But it did not bother me in the slightest."

"What?" If it's possible to die of embarrassment, I'm about to go down.

"It was a sign that you trust me enough to sleep deeply in my arms. You know that I will protect you and that I would never hurt you. You honored me with your snores and your drooling."

A short puff of air escapes me in a laugh. "My snores and drooling *honored you?*"

"Yes."

"You're serious?" I ask, just to be sure.

He nods beneath my hand. "You allowed yourself to be in a highly vulnerable state around me. A male you only recently met. You entrusted me with your life. And I vow that I will continue to prove to you that I am worthy of this trust you have placed in me.

I will honor you, cherish you, treasure you, protect you… and I will do the same for our fledglings if you decide to choose me as yours."

My heart flutters in my chest. He says these things so matter-of-factly, but they are the most romantic words I've ever heard. *And I read a lot of romance novels.*

I'm completely taken aback. I try to think of something to say, but the words get stuck in my throat.

"You talk in your sleep as well."

My head jerks back. "What did I say?"

"You asked if I was real." He gently cups my cheek. "When I told you that I was, you fell back to sleep."

Tears stings my eyes. I know it's an irrational fear to think that I could still be dreaming, but I can't help it. Not after all the things that I've experienced over the past few months were worse than any nightmare I've ever had.

"Rest, my Ashaya," he whispers as he tightens his wings around me to keep me warm. "We have a long journey ahead of us."

Closing my eyes, I allow myself to completely relax for the first time in I'm not even sure how many months, since I was taken. As I fall away into sleep, I know without a doubt that I'm safe in his arms.

CHAPTER 14

RONIN

When I wake in the morning, Kyra is nestled securely in my wings. Her palms rest on my chest and her head is on my shoulder. I listen to the light sound of her snoring and my heart swells with pride at her trust in me.

She is deep in sleep, and I am loath to wake her, but I know that I must. The sun has risen outside and we must travel as far as we can while it is light before we find somewhere to shelter for the night.

"Kyra," I whisper softly.

She responds by nestling closer into my chest and tucking her head under my wings.

"Kyra," I speak her name again, this time a bit louder.

She pokes her head up, blinking sleepily at me. "It's morning already?"

I nod. "We must leave. It is best to travel as far as we can before nightfall."

Kyra stretches and yawns loudly. When I unwrap my

arms and wings from her form, she shivers slightly as she stands. "It's too bad we couldn't have landed on some sort of tropical paradise world," she murmurs to herself as she rubs her arms.

"There is a moon near my home world that has a tropical climate. It is a popular place for travel due to its temperate weather and sandy beaches. I will take you there someday if you'd like."

Her lips curve up in a stunning smile. "I'd like that." She turns her gaze toward the cavern entrance and the snow falling outside. "It will give me something to look forward to while we're braving the cold."

I have rescued many slaves during my time as a commander in the Mosauran Empire, and I know many of them never truly recover from everything they have gone through.

The slavers break their slaves through torture and beatings. I can only imagine what Kyra must have endured. Her injuries, according to Healer Khiran, suggest she was beaten many times.

To hear the optimism in her voice and see the smile on her face speaks of great strength of will. The slavers tried to break my Ashaya, but they failed. She is strong, and I have never admired anyone as much as I do her. I only hope that she will find me worthy enough to remain at her side for the rest of our days.

After we pack up our belongings in the emergency bag, she slings the pack over her shoulders and follows me, without hesitation, to the cavern ledge. I take one more moment to check that she is bundled up against the cold before shifting into my draken form.

Kyra carefully climbs up onto my back and we take to the skies. I swoop down to the valley below, flying just above the tree line.

Knowing that there are potential enemies on this world, like the A'kai and the Lycaons, I want to draw as little attention as possible to our presence. Staying close to the woods minimizes how many can see us from off in the distance.

Kyra and I talk back and forth along our journey. I love that we can communicate with our minds. Dark clouds gather up ahead, but I suspect the storm they herald is far enough away to not be a problem. Not yet, anyway. Tomorrow may be different if it has not yet moved on.

"Is that the direction we're going?" Kyra asks, and I know she is worried about the storm as well.

"Yes. But perhaps it will have moved on before we reach it. I—"

"Did you see that?" Kyra's voice fills my head in alarm. *"There's something to the left. It's some sort of reflection."*

I dip my left wing and turn in that direction, scanning the forest for any sign. *"What did it look like?"*

"I only caught a glimpse of something shiny. But I don't see it now."

As I scan the trees, something glints in the light. *"I see it."*

I make a wide arc out over the trees, trying to get a better look without approaching directly. It could be a trap, and I will not make it easy for an enemy to target us.

We draw closer, and I notice several downed trees surrounding what appears to be a wrecked ship. From the size and shape, I suspect it may have been some sort of trade vessel.

"A ship," Kyra says. *"Is it one of yours?"*

"No. This one looks like a private glider. At most, it could probably carry a crew of four or five."

From the heavy amount of rust visible on the hull, I suspect it has been here for quite some time.

As we circle over the wreckage, I do not see any signs of recent activity, but I know looks can be deceiving. I flare my nostrils, scenting the wind for any signs of someone nearby, but sense nothing.

We pass directly overhead, and my eyes widen when a golden reflection catches my attention. Several l'sair crystals are spread out on the ground, beside the hatch. This must have been a trade vessel, carrying this precious commodity.

"This ship was transporting l'sair crystals."

"What are those?"

"They are used to power engines, cities... entire worlds. But more importantly, they can provide light and warmth." I think of Kyra's shivering this morning. We could use these when we make shelter each night. *"We should gather some for our journey."*

"All right," she replies. *"Let's go down there."*

"I will find a spot for you away from the ship in case anyone is there. Then, I will check out the wreckage and—"

"No," she states firmly. *"I'm going with you. We're a team, remember? You need someone to watch your back."*

Clenching my jaw, I nod slightly. *"Fine. But stay close to me."*

I hate the idea of her being in any danger, but she is right. She has a blaster and it would be safer for me to have someone 'watching my back,' as she says.

I circle a few times and then carefully touch down. It goes against my every instinct to have her here, but I try to convince myself that this is better. If she is close, we can leave quickly at the first sign of any danger.

CHAPTER 15

KYRA

As soon as we land, Ronin lowers himself so I can climb off his back. He shifts into his two-legged form in the blink of an eye. He immediately steps in front of me as he scans the wreckage for danger.

I peer out from behind him, gazing at the ruined vessel and wondering about its former occupants. The hull is rusted and heavily dented in several places, probably from the crash. The airlock door hangs partially open, and as Ronin carefully pulls it back, I can see nothing but darkness inside.

His nostrils flare as he tips up his head, scenting the wind. He turns back to me. "No one is here and they haven't been for a long time."

I notice the l'sair crystals scattered outside the door, as if someone had to leave in a hurry. Ronin must draw the same conclusion because he turns his head out to gaze at the surrounding forest with piercing eyes. "Someone had to abandon this place quickly and they never returned."

"What do you think happened?"

"Perhaps a predator or—" He stops short and opens the hatch just enough to reach inside. He pulls out a tablet and dusts it off before pressing a button on the side.

The screen blinks and flickers to life. I can't make out any of the symbols that flash across the screen but it seems Ronin can as he moves through the various menus.

I reach up and feel the small nub of metal behind my left ear. It seems the translator the slavers gave me only works for language and not writing. "What does it say?"

"It is a log." He taps the screen and an alien appears.

My head jerks back as I study the image of a strange-feline looking alien. With pointed-cat-like ears, his nose is a bit broader than a Terran's and his body is covered in a short layer of black and white fur in a tiger-stripe pattern. His yellow cat eyes stare into the screen. He opens his mouth to speak, but the image freezes.

Ronin growls low and taps the display, but nothing happens. "The processor must be corroded."

"What is he?" I ask, pointing at the image.

"They are called Craven."

"Are they good? Or bad?"

He turns to me. "They are known to be aggressive and very territorial." He scans the woods. "They are also excellent hunters. Something either chased them away, which is unlikely, or they are dead."

Fear snakes down my spine. "What do you think happened?"

"I do not know." He pulls the hatch completely open. "Stay close behind me."

I nod, and then follow him into the darkness.

Ronin presses a hand to a small panel on the wall and interior lights flicker on. They are dim, but it is enough to help me see where I'm going as he leads me through a narrow corridor.

The metal walls, floor and ceiling feel claustrophobic, and I'm glad when Ronin opens a set of doors revealing the bridge. It's rather spacious compared to the hallway. I'm surprised by how most of the panels and displays are either broken or pulled apart as if the Craven were trying to fix them.

We cross the bridge and go through another set of doors into a slightly wider hallway with two doors on either side. Ronin opens the first set, revealing a room with a bed only big enough for one person and a small desk and chair.

These must be crew quarters.

We continue, peering inside each doorway, but find no recent signs of anyone. Several personal items—pictures and clothing—are still here. It looks like their owners might return at any moment. I'm pretty sure that whatever happened, it caught the Craven by surprise and it was fast.

A door at the end of the hallway opens into a bathroom and shower area. Ronin presses a panel, and to our surprise, a wand appears in the corner and begins spraying hot water.

"The water recyclers appear to be in working order," he murmurs more to himself than to me.

I run my hand beneath it, reveling in the feel of the warm water on my skin. As much as I'd love a hot shower, I know we need to finish our search for supplies and move on.

We leave the shower area and find another set of doors that lead to what appears to be the crew mess. Three plates with rotting food and half-empty glasses sit on one of the tables.

These guys definitely left in a hurry.

Ronin opens a cabinet and finds several packets of emergency food and water. He fills our bag with the supplies and then turns to me. "We can retrieve more blankets and perhaps some extra clothing to keep you warm."

I nod, and we continue our search by returning to crew quarters and going through the closets. We find two large, black fur blankets. Ronin drapes one around my shoulders, and I revel in the newfound warmth as he tightens my belt around it to keep it in place. "How is that?" he asks, smoothing a hand down the sides to make sure they are secure.

I smile at that small bit of extra care he gives me. "Perfect. Thank you."

When we head back to the bridge, Ronin presses a button and two metal panels slide apart, revealing a massive viewscreen. The sky outside is much darker than when we first entered and Ronin's eyes widen as a flash of lightning streaks across black clouds, rolling overhead as snow begins to fall heavier outside.

"The storm must have caught up to us," I tell him.

"It was moving much faster than I thought. We will have to shelter here until it passes." He turns to me. "Stay here. I will gather some of the l'sair crystals from outside and finish a quick sweep of the ship."

I want to argue that I should go with him, but he turns to me. "I will call if I need help. Because of the tight quarters, it will be much faster if I search the ship alone."

It makes sense. The corridors on this vessel are rather small. "All right."

He leaves, and I wait on the bridge. A low rumble sounds along the hull that I figure must be him closing and sealing the hatch shut. I palm my blaster at my hip to reassure myself. Whatever happens, at least I'm not helpless. Not like I was when I was a slave.

After what feels like an eternity, but I'm sure was less

than ten minutes, Ronin returns. "The ship is secure. We are safe here for the night."

My shoulders sag forward in relief. A smile quirks my lips when I remember the shower and the crew quarters. "Is it safe to use the shower?"

He nods.

"All right. Bath first, then we'll eat."

He leads me back to the shower room and turns on the water. I wait a moment for him to leave, but he remains rooted in place, staring at me expectantly. "You may shower first if you wish."

I frown. "Are you... going to stay in here?"

"Yes. It is safer if we remain together."

"Uh... but I need to remove my clothes to shower."

He turns his back. "I will not gaze upon your nude form. You have my word."

I glance at the stalls that have what I recognize are the alien version of toilets. "I need a bit more privacy than that. Can you wait outside the door instead?"

"Of course." He turns to me. "I will be right outside if you need me."

Once he leaves, I make quick use of the facilities. After that, I peel off my layers of clothing and step into the shower. I tip my head back, reveling in the sensation of the warm water on my skin, feeling the muscles of my shoulders relax as the heat seeps into me.

When I'm finished, I realize that I have nothing to dry off with. I carefully lift the fur blanket in front of me to hide my naked body and gently call through the door. "Ronin?"

The doors slide open and Ronin's eyes widen. The purple color of his cheeks turns even darker as his gaze travels over my form. "Yes?"

I'm mostly covered, but I thought his people were used to nudity. I'm surprised that he seems embarrassed.

His pupils are wide. Only a thin rim of gold is barely visible around the edges, and I realize it's not embarrassment, it's attraction as he gazes at me.

My face flares with heat. "I need something to dry off with."

Numbly, he nods and then steps around me to push open a cabinet near the shower. He pulls out a towel and hands it to me. "Thank you."

CHAPTER 16

RONIN

I know that I should not stare at her, but I cannot force myself to look away. Her dark brown hair hangs down around her shoulders. Small rivulets of water travel down her body, gathering in the 'v' of her chest, between her breasts, before disappearing beneath the fabric she covers herself with.

Mosauran females do not have prominent breasts, and I have never given much thought to this part of the body. Yet, as I notice the two rounded globes just barely visible above the fur blanket wrapped around her form, I find myself oddly fascinated by them.

I force myself to turn my back to Kyra. My stav presses insistently against the inside of my mating pouch with want to extend. Need burns through me like fire. I long to claim my Ashaya. To join our bodies as one and give her my mark. But I know I must wait. She has not decided if she wants me yet.

"You can turn around," she says.

Slowly, I turn and find her dressed in my tunic again. I curl my fingers into my palms and hold my hands at my sides, desperate to distract myself from the desire coursing through my veins. I long more than anything to pull her to me. To wrap her up in my arms and—

She shivers slightly, and I quickly pick up the discarded fur and wrap it around her form. "Is that better?"

"Much," she replies with a faint smile.

I gather the rest of her clothing and carry it with us down the hallway. I've already decided upon which room is the cleanest, and I lead her inside. "You may have the bed."

She turns to me. "It's all right. We can share."

Happiness fills my chest. I had hoped she would still wish to sleep with me, and I am glad that she does. I relish the thought of holding her as she sleeps, but I had not wanted to press her if she did not wish to continue as we have the past few nights.

When we lie down for the evening, I turn off the lights. I'm surprised when several glowing dots appear on the ceiling. It takes me a moment to recognize the various star patterns and constellations.

"Whoever had these quarters must have missed home," Kyra says, staring up at the ceiling.

"Yes."

"My dad and I painted stars on my ceiling like this when I was a child." A wistful smile crests her lips. "He taught me all about the stars and the constellations. He's the reason I joined the Terran Space program in the first place."

The smile falls from her face. "I miss them so much."

I wrap my wings even tighter around her. Cupping the back of her head, I pull her close to my chest. "When we leave this world, we will not stop searching until we find them."

"What if we can't leave this place?" She sniffs. "What if

we're stuck here forever?" She lifts her head to me. "If there was a way off, why did you pick up so many distress signals?"

"I do not know." I wish I could promise her that we will find a way to escape this ice world, but I know that I cannot. I can only offer her hope. I cup her chin, forcing her gaze to mine. "I vow that I will do all that I can to find a way for us to leave. But if we cannot, know that I will never stop trying. I will never give up. And whatever happens, I will remain at your side. Always."

A tear slips down her cheek, and I gently brush it away with my thumb. "I did not wish to upset you, my Ashaya."

"You didn't," she whispers. A faint smile tugs at her lips even as her eyes are bright with tears. "Did I mention that you're perfect?"

I love that she thinks this of me. I arch a teasing brow. "I thought you did not want me to become too full of myself."

Kyra laughs softly and it is such a lovely sound.

I smile brightly at her, glad to see her so joyful.

Kyra cups my cheek. "Thank you," she whispers.

"For what?"

"Everything," she murmurs.

Gently, I drop my forehead to hers. "I would see you laugh every day if I could, my Ashaya."

"My parents would have loved you." She grins. "You would have won them over in a heartbeat."

My chest swells with pride. "My mother would already be demanding we have fledglings as soon as possible, even though we've only just met." I laugh. "She is so upset that my sister and I are still unbonded. She is always trying to help us find mates."

"My mom is the same with me and my brothers," she offers. "It's so tiring sometimes. I mean... I would come home from a long trip, and she would already have arranged for me to go on some date with some guy that was a son of one of her friends or... something like that."

Jealousy fills me. I know that Kyra did not know me then, but I hate the idea of another male trying to court her. "And did you... like any of them?"

The question escapes my lips without thinking. I should not have asked because now I am worried her answer will be yes. I know she is not my mate, but I already feel fiercely possessive of her.

"No," she replies, and my shoulders relax. "One of them tried to kiss me even though I ended our date early because I didn't like him."

"Kiss?" I cock my head to the side. "Is that the mashing of mouths that Terrans do?"

"Mashing of mouths?" She laughs heartily. "Well, I guess that's one way to put it."

I arch a brow. "I am most curious about this. I have seen our prince do this with his Terran mate on one of the vid feeds, but I do not understand the purpose."

"There are different types of kissing, but the one you're talking about... it's something intimate that couples do with each other."

My gaze drops to her lips, and I'm already imagining the feel of her mouth against my own. "There are other types of kissing?"

Her eyes search mine a moment before she carefully leans in and gently brushes her lips to my cheek. "This is a kiss." She presses her mouth softly to my forehead. "So is this."

My face heats at her touch as my heart pounds in my chest. Scent is very important to Mosaurans. When we take a mate, we mark them as ours with both our scent and our fangs. With each press of her lips to my skin, it is as if she is marking me in a way... the warmth of her touch, branding me as hers.

She leans in and brushes her lips to mine. The touch so light and yet so intimate that my hearts begin hammering.

Kyra pulls away all too soon, leaving me breathless with anticipation as I wait for what she will do next.

Her warm breath whispers across my skin as her mouth hovers so close to mine it would be easy to lean in and touch my lips to hers once more.

But I wait. It must be her choice to gift me her touch. I will not take it without her permission.

My pulse pounds in my ears as she brushes her lips against mine once more. Her tongue traces lightly along the seam of my mouth, and I open for her.

Gently, we explore each other as her smooth tongue curls around my ridged one. I understand now what this is. It is pure and utter bliss, and when she molds her body to mine, I am lost in sensation.

I run my hands down her form, marveling at the feel of her petal-soft skin beneath the tips of my fingers as she touches me in return.

I thread my fingers through her silken hair as our mouths mesh repeatedly and I stroke my tongue against hers in a sensual give and take. I do not understand how my people have gone so long without this knowledge of kissing. It is wonderful.

Thunder cracks loudly overhead, and we both still and pull away. "That was really loud," she says, worry easily read in her features.

"We are safe in here," I reassure her. "The storm cannot touch us in here."

Another thunderous boom rolls above us, and I cup her chin. I want so much to continue where we left off, but I know she is tired. "Rest, my Ashaya. There is nothing to fear in here from the storm. We are safe," I repeat.

She nods and settles against me. As much as I want to kiss

her again, I will wait for her to initiate this. Already she has gifted me her trust and her touch, and I will not press her for more than she is ready to give.

I start to drift off to sleep, but she begins to stir against me. Gently, I cup her chin, noting that her eyes are still closed.

She must be dreaming again.

Kyra brings her palm to rest on my chest, directly over my heart, and I understand what this is before the question even leaves her lips. "Is this real?" She whispers in her sleep. "Are you really here?"

Gently, I nuzzle her hair and place my hand over hers, on my chest. "This is real, my Ashaya. I am here."

Subconsciously, she touches me often in her sleep like this. It is how she reassures herself that this is not a dream, as she fears.

I press a tender kiss to her forehead and whisper softly. "I will remind you every night that I am here, and that I will never leave you. And I will do this for as long as it takes for you to believe it in your heart, my Kyra."

CHAPTER 17

KYRA

The storm is still raging outside as we try to sleep. We've been here five days and while Ronin is concerned by how long it's been, I'm not.

I feel safe in this place, and part of me wishes we could stay here forever. I know it's only temporary though, but it's nice to be able to relax a bit and not have to constantly worry about our survival. We have everything we need in here. But that same thought makes me wonder even more about what might have happened to the cat-like aliens that were here before us.

Surely they wouldn't have left their ship. Especially not with everything pretty much still working like it does.

I'm completely wrapped up in Ronin's arms and wings. His body is molded against mine, with my back to his chest. Last night, I had another nightmare.

He gently woke me, reminding me that I'm safe and I'm free, reassuring me that this is all real and not just another dream.

It's only been a few days, but I'm already falling for him. If I'm being honest with myself, I've been halfway in love with him since the first day we met. I can't explain it, but I don't feel that I need to. After everything that's happened to me, I'm not going to question something that feels so good and so right.

I want to see where things go with us.

His breathing is still soft and even, and I wonder how he is able to sleep through this storm.

He shifts slightly, and something hard presses against my backside, and I still. Now, I know he's still asleep, because when this happened before, he quickly pulled away, worried that he had upset me.

His arm tightens around my waist, and he presses his nose into my hair. His warm breath in my ear makes a small shiver ripple through me. Not of fear, but of something else entirely.

Heat pools deep in my core, and I replay our kiss in my mind. I loved kissing him. We haven't kissed again after that first time, but I want to. I just… don't know how to ask.

I know he's waiting for me to make a move because I told him I needed time to decide about us and this bond, but I just can't make myself do it. Every time I try, I get flustered and my face turns red with embarrassment. I don't know why it's so hard for me to initiate intimacy, but it is.

Maybe it's because I've never really been intimate with anyone else before.

A soft puff of air parts the hair at the back of my neck as Ronin dips his head to the curve of my neck and shoulder, gently nuzzling at my skin. A low growl rumbles in his chest a moment before something sharp nips at my flesh.

I inhale sharply when I realize it's his fangs on my neck.

He jerks away immediately as if burned.

Quickly, I turn to face him. His eyes are wide as they zero

88

in on my neck. "Forgive me." He runs a hand roughly through his short, dark hair as his cheeks flush a dark hue. "I—I was asleep. I—"

"It's all right." I touch my hand to the spot and feel the indentation of his fangs, but he didn't break the skin. "It doesn't hurt."

He scrubs a hand across his face and looks at me with a pained expression.

"Biting… is that something your people do?" I allow my question to escape unfiltered.

Ronin swallows hard. "It is how we mark our mates."

"So, it's a one-time thing, then? Or does it happen every time you… are intimate with your partner?"

His cheeks are now dark purple. "It happens with the first mating. When the bond is sealed between mates. I… should not sleep with you anymore until you decide if you want me as yours, Kyra."

"Why?" I like sleeping in his arms. He makes me feel safe, cared for… loved…

"Your scent is changing. I believe you are nearing your fertile peak, and it is becoming increasingly difficult to hide my body's responses to your close proximity when we sleep together like this." Guilt flashes behind his eyes. "I nearly marked you in my sleep, Kyra. It would have hurt you. I do not want to risk this. Not anymore."

"I trust you, Ronin. I know you won't hurt me."

He clenches his jaw. "Your trust honors me. Now please… let me honor you by respecting that you need time to decide if you want me as yours."

My first inclination is to tell him that I do. I want to be his mate. But then my mind interrupts with a healthy dose of skepticism. This is all happening so fast. I need to get to know him better. Spend more time with him before making such a huge decision.

My heart argues that we're lost on an ice world with only each other to rely on. Why not jump and worry about the rest later?

After a moment, my mind wins the argument, and I nod. "All right."

I realize this means he'll probably sleep in one of the other rooms now, and I don't like the idea of us being apart. I may feel safe here now, but that doesn't mean there isn't still danger potentially lurking nearby. We still haven't figured out what happened to the Cravens that were here before us. "You can have the bed," I offer, hoping he'll take the hint that I want us to stay in the same room. "I'll sleep on the floor."

"You still wish me to remain here with you?" he asks, and I note the cautious tone of his voice. "Even after I nearly marked you?"

I step forward and take his hand. "I trust you. Besides, I think it's safer if we stay together, don't you?" It's not a complete lie. I *do* believe it's safer. But I also just love being near him and waking up to his smile every morning.

"All right," he agrees.

He retrieves a blanket and pillow from the next room and brings it back in here, arranging it on the floor next to the bed. I notice he places himself directly between me and the door, facing it so that he will be the first person that any intruder encounters if someone tries to break in.

He lies down with his back to me, and I already miss the feel of his arms and wings around my body. But I also understand why he's doing this. And I respect it.

As he settles, I reach out and gently rest a hand on his shoulder. He reaches his hand back to place it atop mine. "Goodnight, Ronin."

"Goodnight, Kyra."

CHAPTER 18

RONIN

When I wake, Kyra is still asleep. It is early outside and the storm is beginning to clear. I walk to the bridge and stare out the viewscreen. The entire forest is blanketed in white. Snow still falls heavily outside, but the sun is now visible through the dark clouds overhead.

I suspect we will be able to leave tomorrow. Although I am eager to reach my people, I cannot deny this has been a nice respite. This ship is easily defendable and I have enjoyed the time I've been able to spend with Kyra.

Every day, I learn something new about her. I admire her strength and her ability to adapt quickly to each situation as it presents itself. She is determined to learn how to read and write in my language. I have begun showing her basic symbols and glyphs on my wristband, and I'm surprised by how much she has already learned.

She is fascinated by our technology as well. When I explained to her that our engineers were able to create our wristbands so that they can expand when we shift forms, she was impressed. I wish I could explain the exact science behind it, but I am a commander, not an engineer.

We've tried several times to use my wristband to make contact with my people, but I cannot get a signal to go through.

As if my very thoughts have summoned her, Kyra appears on the bridge. Her smile falls when she notices the storm is beginning to dissipate outside the viewscreen.

I frown. "You are upset that the weather is clearing."

"I just… this was a nice break from everything, you know. I was getting comfortable here."

She's right. This ship has running water and electricity, soft beds, and more importantly, security.

For now, I remind myself.

I am still concerned about the previous occupants and why they are no longer here. I doubt they would have left this place willingly.

"I was as well," I offer. "But if my people are able to transmit a distress signal, then perhaps they have working technology like we have here."

"I hope so." She smiles. "It's been so lovely having warm water for showers, and a nice comfy bed to sleep in every night."

It is instinct to want to provide the best for one's mate. If we were on Mosaura, I would spare no expense making a home for her that had every possible comfort imaginable. I wish that I could promise her that where we are going is better than here, but I cannot.

I take comfort in the fact that when we find my people, she will be well-protected among my fellow Mosauran warriors.

"When do you think we'll be able to leave?" she asks, interrupting my thoughts.

"Tomorrow morning, perhaps." I glance at our surroundings. "I believe we should begin packing everything we wish to take so we can make an early start if the weather is clear when we awaken."

"I agree."

Together, we make our way through the ship, creating an inventory of items to take with us. I'm surprised when she wishes to only take one extra blanket and fur. I had planned to take at least three.

"Three is too many," she argues. "We can't take that much."

"But you will be cold," I counter.

"I'll manage. Besides, I don't want to weigh you down with so many items when I can make do with less."

Her thoughtfulness touches my heart. A Mosauran female would not care for my comfort in this matter. She would simply expect me to be strong enough to carry whatever she wished. And if I could not, it would be viewed as weakness, and she would likely reject me as a potential mate.

"Carrying a few more blankets is no burden," I tell her. "I want to make sure you are warm for our journey, my Ashaya."

CHAPTER 19

KYRA

Ashaya. Each time he calls me his Ashaya, warmth blooms in my chest. Ronin is so wonderful to me. But I can't help but worry that things might change when we reach his people.

We start folding blankets to place in an emergency bag we found, and my mind conjures all sorts of imagined scenarios.

Ronin told me the others will accept me, but I'm still anxious about meeting them.

"What is wrong?" he asks, pulling me back from my dark thoughts. "You are very quiet today."

He's right. Normally, we talk about anything and everything. "I'm just—" I stop short, trying to think of how to explain, and finally offering, "Thinking about what it will be like when we reach your people."

"You are worried." He cocks his head to the side. "Why?"

"What if they don't like me because I'm different?"

"I do not believe that will be a problem."

"How can you be sure?"

He takes both my hands in his, squeezing them gently. "You do not need to fear, my Ashaya. They will not hurt you."

"I know *you* won't. But anyone else might—" My voice hitches as dark memories flood my mind. I bite my bottom lip to stop its quivering. Tears sting my eyes, but I force myself to blink them back.

I am strong. I've survived things that could have broken me if I'd let them, and I refuse to break now.

Ronin cups my chin, tipping my face up to his. He pulls me into his arms and wraps his wings around me. He drops his forehead gently to my own, and his golden eyes search mine. "My people do not condone slavery. No one will touch you against your will."

"What if—"

"If, for some reason, there is a dishonorable warrior among them, know that I would end him without hesitation if he dared try to harm you. I will die to protect you. Always, my Kyra."

"What did I ever do to deserve you?" I whisper.

A smile tilts his lips. "You ask what you did to deserve me, and I ask the Creator what I did in my life that led me to you." He cups my cheek. "And I desire only to remain at your side for as long as you will allow me."

My heart flutters as his gaze holds mine. "What if I want more?"

His brow furrows softly. "Do you?" he asks, and I note the caution in his voice. As if he is trying to temper his hope.

"Yes," I whisper as I lean in and brush my lips against his in a tender kiss.

His hands slide down to my hips, pulling me close as his wings tighten around me. Not in a way that makes me feel trapped or afraid, but in a way that makes me feel desired and loved.

I wrap my arms around his neck as I stroke my tongue lightly against his, deepening our kiss.

One kiss blurs into the next until I'm not sure where one ends and the other begins. His breath is warm and he tastes of spice, and as his delicious ridged tongue moves against mine, I'm lost in sensation.

This feels right. After everything I've been through, I've decided to not waste a single moment. Ronin makes me happy, and he is everything I could ever want in another person. I love him and I'm not going to hold myself back anymore.

His stav is a hard bar between us and pleasure coils tight deep within. I want him.

There is too much clothing separating us; I want to feel his body against mine. I pull back just enough to undress, and he observes in stunned silence.

Heat scalds my cheeks as his eyes drink in my bare form. "You are beautiful," he rasps. "Perfect in every way."

His arms are at his sides, his fingers flexing and extending as if struggling against the want to touch me. I realize he is waiting for me to choose.

I take his hand, and his gaze holds mine as I carefully guide it to my left breast. He inhales a shaking breath as his palm covers the soft globe. I step closer, resting my hands on his chest as I stretch up on my toes and press my lips to his.

Our kiss is slow and gentle, like his hands, as he carefully traces over my body, as if he's afraid I will break beneath his touch.

He strokes his tongue against mine, and I moan as the tip of his hard and erect stav rests against my abdomen. I break from our kiss to study him.

Ronin's stav is much larger than I imagined it would be, although I have nothing to compare him to. I notice a line of ridges along his shaft, and I wonder how that will feel inside me.

Liquid beads on the tip and then spills over the side, running down my abdomen where he is pressed against me. I reach down and trace my fingers along his thick length, and even more begins to gather on the end to trail down my body.

In the back of my mind, I remember what he said about my fertile peak and how the Terran mate of their prince is carrying their child.

As if sensing my concern, he pulls back slightly. "Our species are compatible." His eyes search mine. "If I take you now, there is a chance you could conceive. There are medical advancements that can prevent this, but until we reach my people, I do not—"

"We can just touch each other for now," I whisper against his lips.

His gaze holds mine, full of desire. "Show me how to touch you, my Ashaya," he whispers. "I long only to please you."

I've touched myself before but this is all new. "I've never done this," I admit.

"Neither have I," he murmurs. Gently, he cups his palm to my breast, and I gasp at the delicious sensation. "We will learn together, my Kyra."

CHAPTER 20

RONIN

A low moan escapes Kyra's lips, and she arches against me as I cup her breast.

My nostrils flare as her arousal thickens the air around us. Her scent is intoxicating and stronger now that she is near her fertile peak. Instinct demands that I fill her with my essence, but I know we must wait. I gently guide her to the bed and lower her onto the furs.

She parts her legs, and I settle between them before I capture her mouth in a searing kiss.

I pull back just enough to trace my lips across her jaw and down her neck to the valley of her breasts. I trace my tongue along the soft globe, and when I reach the hard tip, she gasps.

"Kiss me there," she whispers.

I close my mouth over her breast, laving at the stiff peak as she writhes beneath me. Her fingers trace delicate patterns across my shoulders and down my back. Her touch is fire, and I long to claim her.

Her entire body is so soft and giving. I desire more than

anything to sink deep into her warm, wet heat. Need pulses through me, and I move down her body, longing to taste her sweet nectar on my tongue.

I smooth a hand along her inner thigh, gently parting her to my gaze. I lift my eyes to hers. Her entire body is flushed in arousal. "May I taste you?"

She nods, and I dip my head between her thighs and drag my tongue lightly through her folds.

Kyra moans, arching up off the bed when I reach a small nub at the apex. "That's really sensitive," she breathes. "Keep doing that."

Encouraged by her words and her response, I concentrate my tongue on this area, teasing around the tender flesh.

Her fingers dig into my hair as if trying to hold me in place. She writhes beneath my tongue, and I band an arm over her hips to hold her still as I continue to taste her.

I love how responsive she is to my touch, and the taste of her nectar is incredible on my tongue.

"Ronin," she barely manages. "I think I'm going to—"

She arches up, her body tensing beneath me a moment before she cries out my name as she finds her release, flooding my tongue with her essence.

When I move back up her body, she's breathless and panting. She reaches between us and I groan as she wraps her hand around my stav. She cannot quite reach all the way around me, but it is sensitive nonetheless, and I worry that I will release if she does not stop.

Her eyes search mine as she cups my cheek. "Ronin, you didn't—"

"I want only to give you pleasure, my Ashaya." I brush my lips to hers. "Mine can wait."

She gently strokes my stav, and a low growl builds in the back of my throat as desire pulses through my veins. "I want you to feel as good as I do," she whispers. "I want to try tasting you."

I still. I have never heard of such a thing. My brow furrows. "This is common among your people? For a female to take a male's stav in their mouth?"

She nods and gently guides me onto my back. "You'll have to tell me what feels good because I'm not sure what I'm doing, but I think I understand the basics."

I touch her face, searching her eyes. "Are you sure you wish to do this? I do not want you to feel that you must do this because I gave you pleasure, Kyra."

A smile crests her lips. "I want to do this, Ronin."

She presses a kiss to my mouth and then moves down my body to my stav. She carefully grips my shaft, and I groan as she takes the tip into her mouth.

Warm heat envelopes me, and I growl low in my chest, struggling to hold back my release. I do not want to spend my essence in her mouth. I do not think she would want that.

Her tongue swirls across the tip of my stav, and it takes every bit of my control to remain still beneath her attentions.

My claws extend, digging into the bed beside me as I desperately try to hold back when all I want to do is thrust into her mouth.

Each swipe of her delicate tongue around my stav is the most exquisite torture. I run my hands through her hair, careful to retract my claws so I do not hurt her. "Kyra," I rasp. "You must stop. I am too close."

Instead of listening, she continues.

Heat builds deep within, and I pant heavily as I fight to hold myself back.

I'm so close to the edge, I know I will not last. "Kyra, stop!" I cry out.

She lifts her head away.

Primal instincts rush through me. In one swift motion, I

pull her body up even with mine and roll her beneath me. I grip my stav as my release erupts from the tip, covering her chest and abdomen with thick, viscous ropes of my seed, marking her with my essence.

I stare down at her, panting heavily. Her gaze holds my own as she takes my hand and spreads my essence across her body and even her breasts. "Mine," I growl as I study her skin, glistening with my release. My nostrils flare at our combined scent.

She cups the back of my neck and pulls my lips down to hers as she whispers against them. "Yours."

CHAPTER 21

KYRA

As I lie in bed with Ronin, I trace my fingers across the soft, leathery folds of his wings.

"What are you thinking, my Ashaya?" he asks softly.

"That I wish we could stay here forever."

"I do too." He drops his forehead gently to mine. "But we will be safer with my people than we are out here alone."

"I know." I rest my palm on his chest. "It's just... this is the first time in I'm not even sure how long that I've been happy. And I guess I'm just worried that it could end."

He cups my chin. "When we find my people, if you are not happy there, I will bring you back here, if that is what you wish."

"You would do that for me?"

"You are my heart. I would do anything for you," he murmurs. "If you desire to carve a life out here, I want only to remain at your side. The place we choose to do that matters not to me, as long as you are there."

Just when I think he could not be more perfect, he goes and says something like this. "I love you, Ronin. My perfect, Mosauran warrior."

He leans in and captures my mouth in a tender kiss. "Yours," he agrees. "Always."

When morning comes, we pack everything we can fit into two emergency bags. Ronin insists upon bundling two furs over my clothing for warmth. It makes me feel as if I'm twice my size, but I don't care. At least it's warm.

I tuck the blaster into my belt and we make our way to the airlock. He carefully turns the latch and pushes the door open. The metal hinges groan loudly as it swings out.

When we step outside, I lift my gaze to the sky. Dark clouds spread out above us, punctuated by the soft light of the sun overhead. Wisps of snow twirl through the air. The tiny flakes stick to my hair and clothing.

A cold wind blows through the forest, nipping at my exposed skin and making me shiver slightly. Ronin turns a worried gaze to me. "Do you need more layers?"

"I'll be fine," I reassure him. "I think I just got used to being warm these past few days in the ship."

Seemingly satisfied by my answer, he turns his gaze out to the forest, scanning the trees for any signs of danger.

Something flashes in the distance. I open my mouth to alert him, but stop as a low growl rumbles deep in his chest. Whatever it is, his head is turned in that direction. He saw it as well.

"Get behind me," he whispers urgently.

I do as he says. He spreads his wings wide as if to shield me from danger. "We are being hunted."

My heart stops and fear trickles down my spine as I remain completely still.

Lightning fast, Ronin shifts into his dragon form. He

grips me in his front paw and then leaps into the air. Beating his wings furiously, he climbs above the trees.

A blast of light zips past us, and he releases a bellowing roar of anger.

My stomach twists in a violent knot as two more blasts of light erupt from the woods, heading straight for us.

Ronin dips his left wing, barely missing the hit. Several more bright lights explode from the trees as Ronin dips and weaves, trying to dodge each one, but there are too many.

He twists, shielding me from another blast, roaring in pain as it slams into his left side. The smell of burned flesh fills my nostrils as he struggles to flap his left wing to keep us aloft.

"Kyra," he speaks in my mind. *"When I tell you to run, you must not hesitate."*

"Run? Where?"

He folds his wings and dives for the ground, extending them at the last second before we fall below the tree line, catching the current and gliding out over the forest.

His chest heaves beneath me, and I know it is taking all his strength to remain aloft. *"Ronin, how badly are you hurt?"*

Panic tightens my chest when he doesn't answer. Three more blasts of light zip past us, barely missing his other wing.

I pull the blaster from my belt and shoot blindly behind me, hoping to hit whoever is attacking us. *"Who's after us?"*

"A'kai," he barely manages. *"You must run while I hold them off."*

The ground races toward us, and he flaps his wings furiously, struggling to control his landing.

"I won't leave you."

"You must!"

He slams into the ground, dust and rock exploding

beneath his weight as he digs his other three paws into the earth to stop our forward momentum.

Shakily, he sets my feet on the ground, his golden eyes meeting mine full of worry before he spins back in the direction of our attackers. *"Run, Kyra! Now!"*

"No!"

"Run!" he cries out in his mind.

Several blasts of light rush toward him, and he spreads his wings wide to shield me. A thunderous roar rips from his throat as two of them slam into his chest.

He collapses to the ground, breathing heavily, and I rush out in front of him, firing repeatedly into the woods.

A piercing cry rings out, telling me I've hit someone, so I keep shooting, praying I get them all.

"Kyra," he barely manages. *"You must leave before it is too late."*

"I'm not going to abandon you, Ronin."

A man bursts through the dense bramble, racing toward me with lightning speed. His long white hair flies out behind him, revealing green skin and two sharply pointed elf ears. His eyes are obsidian black, and his fangs are bared as he races toward us. He raises his blaster, but I fire two more shots.

The man spins away, but I fire another, hitting him square in the chest. I watch in triumph as he crumples to the ground.

Another man comes up behind him, followed by four more.

I take careful aim, steadying my breathing and pushing down my fear as my training kicks in and I force myself to focus on the targets in front of me. I can do this. I have to. Ronin is counting on me.

I fire off two shots, hitting one of the other men before sending another two rounds their way.

Ronin leaps up behind me, still in his dragon form. His tail loops around my waist, jerking me back behind him as he sends a stream of fire arcing out at our enemies.

One of the men releases a pain-filled scream as the flame engulfs him entirely. The other two fire their blasters again and Ronin only has time to avoid one, taking another hit to his side.

I rush out from behind him, firing again, but I miss.

Ronin's entire form is shaking as he stands protectively beside me. He can't take another hit. It will kill him. I'm sure.

Another arc of light heads for him, and I jump in front of it.

Pain explodes across my left side, throwing me back. I slam to the ground, forcing the air from my lungs. I draw in several deep breaths, struggling to breathe as darkness closes in around the edges of my vision.

Ronin's thunderous roar fills the air, and he moves in front of me, throwing his large wing over my body as the world goes black.

CHAPTER 22

KYRA

As my mind slowly comes back into awareness, myriad images fill my thoughts as my memories return.

I jerk up to sitting and gasp when I don't recognize my surroundings. Black metal lines the floors, walls, and ceiling. The faint smell of antiseptic fills my nostrils as my gaze sweeps over the room.

A monitor at the end of my bed displays an outline image of my body, flashing red in warning as my heart races in my chest.

A door opens across the way, and I inhale sharply as an A'kai with short, white hair starts toward me. The pointed tips of his ears stick up through the slightly disheveled strands, and his glowing green eyes fix me with a piercing stare.

Fear rips down my spine, and I twist, falling over the side of the bed and onto the floor.

"Stop!" he commands.

I push myself to my feet, but my legs are so weak, I stumble forward, dropping to the ground. Desperate, I search for anything I can use as a weapon, but find nothing.

"Stop!" he says again, rushing toward me. "I am not going to hurt you."

Ronin's warnings about the A'kai fill my mind, and I scramble backward, slamming into a glass cabinet. Instinct kicks in, and I slam my fist to the glass front, shattering it. I grit my teeth against the pain as I grasp a large shard in my palm, holding the sharp, jagged edge out before me, threateningly. "Where is Ronin?"

"The Mosauran?"

I nod.

"He is in a holding cell. He—"

"Take me to him," I demand. "Now."

"My name is Thalen. I am a Healer." He holds his hands up in mock surrender. "I *am not* your enemy. I am trying to help you."

"Why should I believe you?" I narrow my eyes. "I've been warned about your kind."

"I snuck back into the compound to help you. I'm on your side," he insists. "If the commander were to catch me in here, he would execute me."

"Why?"

"I *do not* have time for this," he grinds out. Without warning, he charges toward me with inhuman speed. I lunge to the side but not fast enough.

He moves behind me, gripping my wrist so I can't cut him with the glass, and locking his other arm around my waist, pinning my free arm to my side. He lifts me off the ground effortlessly and whispers in my ear. "If I wanted you dead, you would be. Now, drop the glass. You are hurting yourself."

Anger twists deep inside me. "Why do you care if I harm myself?"

"Because I have already told you. I am not your enemy, Terran." He growls in my ear. "If you want to escape here alive, you must trust me."

"Take me to Ronin."

"I will," he replies. "But first, drop the glass."

I open my hand, and it falls to the floor, shattering at my feet.

He sets me on the nearest bed and hands me a cloth. "Hold this to your palm while I get the tissue regenerator." He casts a nervous glance at the door. "We must hurry before we are caught."

He moves to another cabinet and pulls out some sort of scanning device. He grips my wrist and pulls the cloth away.

Blood pools across the jagged cut on my palm, dripping onto the floor. His nostrils flare and his eyes turn raven-black as his fangs extend.

I jerk my hand, trying to pull it away, but he holds it tight. "I will not hurt you," he says thickly. "Forgive me. The scent of your blood triggers my instincts."

"What instincts?" I ask.

His feral gaze flicks up to mine. His eyes swirl back to glowing green before he answers. "The instinct to feed. My kind are blood drinkers."

Panic ripples through my veins.

"I will not harm you," he repeats. "You have my vow."

Given what Ronin told me about their kind, I'm not sure that actually means anything, but I don't have a choice right now. I have to trust him.

CHAPTER 23

KYRA

Thalen's glowing green eyes dart again to the door. "We have to hurry before we are discovered." He runs the regenerator over my injury, mending the tissue before my eyes. "What is your name?"

"Kyra." I study him warily. "Why are you helping me?"

He clenches his jaw. "My friend escaped with one of your kind. Perhaps you have seen him." His gaze locks on mine. "His name is Erolas. I helped him get away with his Terran mate—Mina."

"I haven't seen anyone else besides the men who attacked us." I frown. "Are you sure you saw another Terran?"

He nods. "Several of your kind crashed here not long ago with more of my people."

"Where are they?" Hope fills me. "What happened to them?"

"Some have been rescued by the Mosaurans and the V'lo-ryns. But there are two here, besides you, that were captured a few days ago."

"How do you know this?"

"I—"

The front door pushes open and fear rips up my spine as another A'kai walks in.

He stops abruptly in his tracks, his glowing, green eyes widening. "Thalen? What are you doing here? We thought you were dead."

"It is a long story, Maloryn." Thalen positions himself protectively in front of me. "Are you going to turn us in?"

The other A'kai cocks his head to the side. He is heavily armed. The hilt of a dagger is tucked into the long braid of white hair that hangs down his back. Three more blades are sheathed at his belt, beside his blaster. "No," he states firmly. "I will not."

The tense set of Thalen's shoulders relaxes. "Will you help me then?"

He tips up his chin. "What do you need me to do?"

"Take me to the Mosauran and the rest of the Terrans. We must help them escape."

"And where will you go after that?" Maloryn narrows his eyes. "Do you think the Mosaurans will take you in when Commander Dural hunts you down?"

Thalen clenches his jaw. "That is my hope."

Maloryn scoffs. "They are more likely to end you than offer you shelter, brother."

"Then I will go to the V'loryns," Thalen says. "They will—"

"Their Commander—Vorek—will execute you just as surely as Dural would. Vorek has a Terran mate as well and will not tolerate an A'kai anywhere near her. They are deeply possessive and protective of their mates, and he will consider you a threat to her safety. You *know* this." His gaze darts to me and then back to Thalen. "So, I am asking you now: What is your plan?"

Thalen meets his gaze evenly. "I came here to rescue the Terrans. If I can free the Mosauran, he might be able to help us all escape."

"I understand you wanting to get away from Commander Dural," Maloryn says. "Power has driven him mad. But why did you and Erolas risk everything for a Terran female?" He studies me with a predatory gaze. "What is so special about them?"

"The Terran female was Erolas's Fated One—his *Sy'nan*." Thalen swallows hard. "And one of the Terrans being held here now… I recognized her as mine."

His head jerks back, and he blinks several times. "Truly? Your Sy'nan is a Terran?"

"Yes." He clenches his jaw. "Now will you help me free them, or not, Mal?"

He dips his chin in a solemn nod. "I will help you. But you must hide for now while I figure out our next move."

"Where will we hide?" I ask.

Maloryn looks at me. "I was *talking* to Thalen. *You* must remain here and pretend to still be unconscious."

"What if someone discovers that I'm not?" I counter.

He arches a brow. "I am the only Healer here now that Thalen has been gone. No one else comes in the Med Center unless they are injured."

I glance at Thalen. We only just met, but I trust him more than I do Maloryn. Thalen, at least, stood in front of me, ready to defend me if his friend had said he was going to turn us in.

"I will be nearby," Thalen says. He looks at Maloryn. "Thank you, my friend."

Thalen slips through a door in the wall behind the row of beds. Maloryn turns to me. "Lie down," he commands. "If anyone enters, they must think you are still asleep."

I lie down as he instructs. Maloryn stands over me, typing

a series of commands into the display next to my medical bed. "Thank you for helping us," I tell him. "I—"

"I am doing this for Thalen. Not you," he grumbles. "He is my mentor and my friend." He narrows his eyes. "You do not understand the risk he is taking to free you. If he is caught, he will be executed without trial. Commander Dural does not forgive those who disobey."

"What about you?" I ask. "Aren't you worried the commander will find out you helped us?"

He clenches his jaw. "The debt I owe Thalen is worth the risk to my life."

I blink several times, surprised by his answer. "Why?"

"If not for him, I would still be an indentured."

"A what?"

"On our homeworld—A'kaina—if you are an orphan, you are given over into indentured servitude when you come of age. It is how you pay back the Empire for the cost of their care since you had no parents to take on this responsibility. It is nearly impossible to ever pay the debt to buy your freedom."

"How did you do it?"

"Thalen and Erolas paid my debt."

I wait for him to continue, wanting to know more, but he says nothing. Despite his cold demeanor, it is easy to read the pain behind his glowing green eyes before he turns away, pretending to focus on something else.

"Will your Mosauran mate help us?"

"Yes." I frown. "How did you know he was my mate?"

His nostrils flare, and he wrinkles his nose in disgust. "You stink of each other."

"You've seen him?"

He releases an impatient sigh as if my question were stupid. "Of course, I have. I am the Healer on this compound.

It was my job to assess both of you when you were brought in."

My heart stutters. "Is he all right? How badly was he injured? Will he—"

"His kind are very resilient," he replies coldly. "I treated his wounds, and I am excellent at my job. He will live. Now, close your eyes. And if anyone walks in you must remain silent and still." He turns a sharp gaze to me. "I *will not* allow Thalen to be killed because of you. Do you understand, Terran?"

I nod.

"You are fortunate you are here," he adds. "And not being fed on like the rest of them."

My heart stops, and I draw in a shaking breath. "You mean—" My breath hitches. "Your people are drinking their blood?"

He arches a brow. "The Commander is, at least. I've heard he will not share them even with the other officers. Apparently, your blood is something of a delicacy."

Ice floods my veins. "Are you sure they're still... alive?"

"Yes. The Commander wants to keep them around as long as possible. Especially since he enjoys how they taste."

He turns to walk away, but I grip his forearm, stopping him. His head whips toward me with an incredulous look on his face as he pulls his arm from my gasp. "Do *not* touch me," he growls.

"If Thalen weren't here, would you even be helping us?"

I'm pretty sure I already know the answer, but I want to be sure. I need to know how closely I need to watch this guy.

Instead of giving me a direct response, he says, "Thalen asked for my help, so I am giving it. My honor demands nothing less. I would not betray him in this."

Good to know. So as long as Thalen is alive, and on our

side, Maloryn is too. But if anything happens to Thalen... I doubt he'd bother to help us.

"Now, rest," he commands. "I must go to your Mosauran and see what kind of plan I can devise to aid in your escape."

A thunderous roar echoes from outside, chilling me to the bone as I recognize its pitch. "That's Ronin." My voice quavers as pain stabs at my chest. "They're hurting him."

"Yes," Maloryn replies. "The Commander enjoys torturing prisoners."

"Please," I plead. "Can you take me to him?"

He purses his lips. "It is too dangerous. Right now, the only thing keeping you from being the Commander's new favorite pet is the fact that he believes you are still in here, recovering and unconscious."

I meet Maloryn's gaze evenly. "I *need* to see Ronin."

"Are you mad?" he asks incredulously.

"Please. If we're going to escape this place, we need him. And I guarantee you he will not help you unless he knows that I'm all right."

"Fine. But you must do as I say." He points a stern finger at me. "Do you understand?"

Hope flares in my chest. "Yes."

CHAPTER 24

RONIN

"What are the codes for the shield to your compound?" Commander Dural's glowing green eyes are full of rage as he holds up the lash. Dark blood stains his short, white hair, his uniform, and his pale green skin. He wipes a hand across his face and licks the blood from his palm. "Tell me, and I will stop your torture. If you do not, I will feed upon you again once we are finished here."

He circles me, narrowing his eyes. My wrists are bound and my arms are tied, and spread wide between two posts in the center of their compound.

Several A'kai warriors walk past us, glaring at me in disgust. They hate my kind as much as I detest theirs.

"I do not know them," I grind out. "I already told you. I crashed here several days ago in an escape pod. I am not from this Mosauran compound you seek."

"Lies," he snarls.

Lightning fast, he moves behind me. The whip burns

across my flesh with a sharp crack, ripping into my scales as he deals out two more lashes. My nostrils flare at the scent of blood. Warm liquid trickles down my body, and obsidian blood pools in the snow beneath my feet.

My entire back is on fire, pain searing across every nerve ending where my scales are torn open and bleeding.

My muscles are tense with want to shift into my draken form and burn this place to ash. But the dull ache in my shoulder reminds me that to shift would only result in my death. The implanted chip is designed to explode if my body tries to change forms.

If my hands were free, I'd dig it out with my claws. But I cannot. Commander Dural has my wrists bound, rendering me incapable of much movement.

My thoughts turn to Kyra. "Where is the Terran female?" I grit through my teeth as the lash stings again over my shredded scales. "Tell me!"

I have not told them she is my mate. To do so might put her in even more danger than she already is. If they thought they could use her against me, they are right. There is nothing I wouldn't do to keep her from harm.

"You seem to care a great deal for one not of your race," Commander Dural says darkly. "Strange for a Mosauran," he muses. "I'd thought your people did not believe in mixed species pairings."

"We do not," I growl. "Now, let me go, or I vow that I will end you."

"And how exactly do you plan to do that?" He smirks. "You are my prisoner, not the other way around, Commander Ronin."

He walks around from behind me, stalking toward me like a predator closing in on its prey. "Tell me what I want to know and I will give her back to you. If you do not, I will take her. I will feed off of your precious female and ravage her mind while I do so."

Murderous rage floods my veins. His people are touch telepaths and they take great pleasure in forcibly entering their victim's minds in the *R'ugol*—the mind rape. I release a thunderous roar. "If you touch her, I will kill you, Dural! I swear it to the Creator!"

"Ah." His lips curl up in a sinister grin. "So she *is* important to you, then."

"Let her go!"

His eyes burn with anger. "Not until you tell me what I want to know. Give me the codes to your compound!"

"I *do not* have them!"

The lash rips across my scales in three successive blows. Unable to stand through the agonizing pain, I drop to my knees. The only thing holding me upright is the bindings on my wrists.

Darkness gathers at the edge of my vision as I struggle to remain conscious. The pain is so intense, I can barely focus.

"Let me go!" I roar. "Now!"

The lash burns across my back with a sharp crack and I fall forward, tumbling away into oblivion.

CHAPTER 25

KYRA

Maloryn fastens a metal collar around my neck and snaps a chain to the side. He tugs on it slightly to test that it's connected properly.

"There," he says. "You look as though you are ready to be presented to the Commander."

I allow my gaze to travel over my reflection in the mirror. I'm dressed in a slave shift that barely covers anything of my body. Maloryn drapes a fur cloak around me for warmth, covering me up, at least.

"I do not like this," Thalen grumbles behind me. "If you are caught, you will have to take her to Commander Dural. He might—"

"I already know the risks." I cut him off. "This is my choice. I have to get to Ronin." I turn to face Thalen. "We need him on board with our plan so we can escape, not just with us, but with the rest of the Terran women. And I know for a fact, he won't help either of you without talking to me first. He doesn't trust your people."

Thalen exchanges a worried look with Maloryn. "I still do not like this."

"She's right," Maloryn says. "And you know it. The Mosauran will not trust us."

My head snaps to him, surprised that he's actually agreeing with me. From the way he talks and looks at me, I get the impression he thinks I'm pond scum.

Maloryn's eyes travel over me, and he wrinkles his nose again in disdain.

I was wrong. He thinks I'm lower than pond scum.

Before Thalen can try and talk me out of this again, I look at Maloryn. "Let's go."

"All right." His gaze practically burns into mine. "Remember: we will have to make this convincing."

Thalen return to his hiding place in the back of the med clinic while Maloryn and I start for the door.

It's dark outside, but the moon offers just enough light that I can see where I'm going.

Several small buildings constructed of dark metal surround us. From the odd size and shape of the panels that are bolted together, I realize that these must be made from the hull of a ship.

I know the early Mars pioneers broke down each vessel when it arrived to build the first colony. It seems the A'kai have done the same here. They used their broken ship to create a compound that serves as their base and their home.

A pair of glowing green eyes moves toward us in the darkness. As it draws closer, I'm able to make out the face and body it is attached to when an A'kai soldier leers at me. "The new one is ready?" He licks his lips. "The Commander will be most pleased with fresh blood."

"Yes," Maloryn replies smoothly. "But first, I must take her to the Mosauran."

The other man's head jerks back. "Why? Do you intend to rile him again? He is finally quiet."

"I am going to try to make him talk… tell us what we want to know," Maloryn explains. "He cares for this female, and I believe this will make him want to cooperate."

The soldier moves closer, studying me with a piercing gaze. His eyes swirl with black as his fangs extend. "I cannot wait to find more of them. I've heard they are delicious."

A chill runs down my spine as he talks so casually about drinking the blood of my people. My thoughts turn to the other women being held here, and I send a silent prayer to whomever may be listening that they are still alive and well.

A pained roar fills the air, and I inhale sharply. It's Ronin. I need to get to him. Now.

A sharp jerk on my collar is Maloryn tugging roughly at my chain, forcing me to follow after him. He's much taller than me, and I'm practically running behind him to keep up as he walks at a brisk pace through the compound.

We reach a clearing, and my heart stops when I see Ronin in the center between two metal columns. His wrists bound and tied to the posts on either side of his body. He's on his knees in the snow, his head hanging forward as his chest rises and falls rapidly with panting breaths.

An A'kai soldier kicks at his side, and Ronin releases an anguished roar.

"Why doesn't he shift?" I whisper, blinking back tears.

"There is a chip in his shoulder, set to explode the moment he tries to change forms."

Horror fills me. "How do you know?"

He turns to me. "Because the Commander ordered me to put it there."

"You monster," I grit through my teeth. "I'll kill you for—"

"Save your anger, Terran." He growls low in his throat. "Use it. Draw on it to lend you strength." His piercing green eyes meet mine, and something flashes behind them. An emotion that I can't quite discern. "You will need it if you are to survive."

Something tells me he knows this from experience. Given what little he's told me of his childhood, I can only imagine it must have been hard. As much as I don't want to pity him, I recognize the pain he tries so hard to hide.

When we reach Ronin, one of the A'kai soldiers moves to kick him again, but Maloryn calls out. "Stop!"

The man halts abruptly, blinking at him in confusion.

"I am here to question this Mosauran, and I must have him conscious to do it."

The soldier nods in agreement.

"Now, leave us."

He dips his chin. "Of course, Healer Maloryn."

Ronin's head hangs down and my heart clenches as we walk around him. His back is torn to shreds and bleeding. The obsidian blood trails down his form, pooling on the ground.

Maloryn unclips my collar and whispers. "Go to him. Tell him the plan. Quickly. We do not have much time."

His eyes dart nervously around us, checking to make sure we're alone.

I rush to Ronin and drop to my knees. I want so much to throw my arms around him, but he's so torn up, I don't want to hurt him. I cup my hands on either side of his face, tipping his head up to mine. His eyes blink open and then widen as he recognizes me. "Kyra," he breathes out my name. "You are here, my Ashaya."

"Yes, my love," I press a tender kiss to his lips. "I'm here, Ronin. I'm here."

"You have to run," he barely manages. "You have to escape."

I shake my head softly as tears fall down my cheeks. "Not without you, my love. We have a plan."

Maloryn walks up behind me, and a menacing growl rips from Ronin's throat. "Get away from her."

Maloryn holds up his hands in mock surrender as Ronin forces himself to stand on unsteady feet. His entire body bristles with rage as he glares at the A'kai. "Let her go," he grits through his teeth. "Now."

"Ronin," I cup his cheek, forcing his attention back to me. "He's here to help us."

Unconvinced, Ronin growls again. "He is A'kai. They are not to be trusted."

"He healed me, Ronin. He and his friend are both Healers. They are going to help us and the rest of the Terrans escape."

Something akin to hope flares behind his eyes, but it's gone too quickly for me to be sure. He levels an icy glare at Maloryn. "Why would you help us?"

"Because I owe a life debt to my friend," he snarls. "*He* is the one who wants to help you. So I am helping him in return."

Ronin's chest heaves with exertion as he struggles to draw in deep breaths. I don't see how he will be able to fly us out of here. Not like this.

"You have to heal him." I look at Maloryn. "Please."

Maloryn sighs heavily, rolling his eyes. "Why do you think I brought this?" He pulls a tissue regenerator from his pocket. "I am a Healer, not an idiot."

Ronin growls. "Do not speak to her in this manner, A'kai. Or I will—"

"Do you want me to heal you or not?" Maloryn snaps.

Ronin grumbles, narrowing his eyes.

"Be quiet," Maloryn hisses. "Both of you, or else we will be caught before we even have a chance to try and get all of you out of here."

"What about you?" I ask, because I realize he never mentioned leaving with us.

"Why would I go with you? What is there for me at the Mosauran compound but certain death." He levels an icy glare at Ronin. "I am right, am I not?"

Ronin remains silent, his own ice-cold stare answering for him. Maloryn is right. The Mosaurans will probably kill Thalen on sight once we reach their compound. I want to tell Ronin that Thalen helped me. Maloryn did too, even though he is only doing it for his friend.

But there isn't time. We have to hurry if we're going to have any chance at escape.

CHAPTER 26

RONIN

Even as the A'kai runs the tissue regenerator over my back, my chest tightens with worry for Kyra. She is everything to me, and I am terrified we'll be discovered and they will hurt her.

I still do not entirely trust this A'kai, but we don't have a choice.

I glance at the buildings all around us. I will burn them to ash if they dare touch her.

Healer Maloryn removes the bindings from my wrist, and I gather Kyra in my arms, pulling her close to my chest.

She embraces me with a strength I did not think her people possessed. "I was so worried about you," she whispers against my chest. "I love you so much. Don't you dare sacrifice yourself for me again, do you understand?"

Maloryn huffs out an exasperated sigh. "We do not have time for this nonsense. We must go."

"Remove the chip from my body," I growl. "Now."

I could try to remove it with my claws, but I would risk setting it off.

The A'kai Healer hesitates a beat. "How do I know you will not end me once I do?"

"You do not," I reply darkly.

"He helped us, Ronin," Kyra interjects. "As much as I dislike Maloryn, and I know he doesn't like me, I don't want to see him dead either. You can't hurt him."

I bare my fangs in an angry snarl. "Yes, I can."

"All right, technically you can," she points out, "but I don't want you to, all right?"

"Fine." I sweep my gaze to Maloryn. "Now, remove this chip." I extend my claws. "Or I will tear it from my flesh and end you."

Maloryn purses his lips. "You really believe threatening me is the way to go with this?"

A deep growl vibrates in my chest as I bare my fangs. "Yes."

CHAPTER 27

RONIN

Maloryn quickly slices a line along my shoulder and extracts the chip. The moment he does, I glare at him. He takes several steps back, holding up his hands. "I helped you. You cannot—"

"Where are the other Terrans?" I snarl. "Tell me. Now."

He points toward a building in the far corner of the compound. "In there. But we must retrieve Thalen from the med clinic first."

"Why?"

"Because they helped us, Ronin," Kyra reminds me. I cup her cheek and press a tender kiss to her lips. My mate's heart is too pure for this world and these vile creatures. "We leave them here," I tell her. "I will not take the A'kai with us."

"No," she states firmly. "Thalen's Fated One is one of the Terrans. We can't separate them."

My head jerks back, and I blink up at the A'kai Healer. "This is truth?"

He nods. "He says one of them is his Sy'nan."

"Fine," I growl. "Lead us to the med clinic."

We slip quietly through the compound and past several buildings until we reach the clinic. As soon as we enter, I point to Kyra's collar. "Remove this," I grind out. "Now."

Maloryn runs a hand through his long, white hair. "We do not have time for this."

"Just do as I command," I grit through my teeth.

He growls and then fumbles with the lock and clasp before finally snapping it open. I pull it off her neck and throw it to the ground. "You will never be collared again."

"You cannot promise her that," Maloryn counters. "We are not safe yet."

Another A'kai with short, white hair comes from the back. Lightning fast, I pull Kyra behind me, flaring my wings to protect her.

"It's all right, Ronin," she calls softly from behind me. "That's Thalen. He helped me, too."

I rake my gaze over his form. "Your Fated One is Terran." I say this as a statement, but it's meant as a question.

"Yes." He clears his throat. "I ask that you take us both with you, along with the other Terran females, back to your compound."

"As I told your Commander before, I am not from the Mosauran compound here."

"Yes, but you are Mosauran and that is your destination, is it not?" Thalen counters.

I nod.

"Then, I ask that you take us there."

"I cannot guarantee your safety once we reach it," I give him the truth.

He clenches his jaw. "I understand. It is a risk I am willing to take. I ask only that you look after my Fated One if something should happen to me. Will you do this?"

I dip my chin. "You have my vow as a warrior."

Maloryn rolls his eyes again. "All of this for a Terran female," he scoffs. "I wish you would not leave on this fool's errand, Thalen. You—"

"You do not understand, Mal," he cuts him off. "Nor do I expect you to. I ask only that you accept my decision in this matter."

Maloryn frowns. "You know I do. I have risked everything to help you, and I will risk even more before this night is done."

So, *this* is the one that he owes a life debt to. This is the reason he is helping us. I watch as he rests a hand on Thalen's shoulder. "I honor my debt and our friendship this night."

His words sound sincere. I no longer believe he will betray us, but I will keep a sharp eye on him anyway.

Now, it's me who is impatient. "We must go."

Maloryn narrows his eyes. "Follow me."

CHAPTER 28

KYRA

Ronin carries me as we make our way through the compound, moving from one shadowed area to the next in an attempt to remain unnoticed. At first, I wanted to argue that I could walk, but he moves so much faster than me and with far more stealth. So do the A'kai.

Maloryn leads us while Thalen trails behind.

As we stake out the building where my people are being held, I turn to Thalen. "Your Fated One... What is her name?"

He swallows hard. "I do not know."

"What do you mean?" I frown. "How could you not know her name?"

"I have never spoken to her."

"What?"

He runs a hand roughly through his hair. "I—"

"Speak truth," Ronin growls. "What is it?"

"I dreamed of her," he reluctantly admits. "I saw her face in a vision, and I felt drawn to come back here after I got separated from Erolas and Mina. Fate called me to her. And when I got here, I saw that she had been captured… that my people already had her here." He clenches his jaw. "And I knew I needed to help her escape."

Maloryn's eyes sweep to Thalen. "You will risk your life for a female you do not even *know*?" He runs a hand roughly through his long, white hair, shaking his head in frustration. "And I am risking my life for this as well."

"I never asked—"

"Yes, you did," Maloryn snaps.

"Quiet," Ronin hisses. "You can fight amongst yourselves later."

Maloryn stares at Thalen, betrayal easily read in his features before he turns his attention back to the building we have to reach. "She had better be worth it," he mutters under his breath.

I look at Thalen. "Let me talk to her. She will not trust you." I glance at all three of them. "Any of you," I add.

Ronin and Maloryn nod. Thalen gives me a pained look before finally agreeing.

CHAPTER 29

KYRA

Maloryn walks in first, checking to make sure it's clear. He's the Healer in this compound, so if he gets caught inside, he can simply say he was there to look in on the Terrans.

The rest of us wait around the corner. Worry twists deep inside me. My entire body is practically shaking with nervous energy. It would be so much easier to leave now, but I would never be able to live with myself if we left those women behind in the hands of these monsters.

I glance at Thalen. The stories of the A'kai, told among other slaves, are only spoken of in hushed whispers because their race is so feared. They are Vampires. Living, breathing monsters that I always thought were make-believe.

I highly doubt the woman he claims is his mate will be accepting of what he is. Especially if she's been held by his people... tortured and fed upon by their Commander.

After what feels like forever, but is probably only a few

137

minutes, Maloryn opens the door and motions for us to come to him.

Quickly and quietly, we slip inside. My jaw drops as soon as I see the women. Lying on a bed in one corner, their wrists and ankles are bound by chains that are attached to the metal wall. Their eyes are closed as if asleep.

"They have been drugged," Maloryn says. "I cannot wake them."

Ronin sets me on my feet, and I rush toward them. Rage builds in my chest as my gaze travels over the several bite marks along their necks and arms. They have been fed upon. Many times.

I don't recognize either of them. One has short, blond hair, and the other has curly red locks. Each of them are terribly thin, and I wonder how long they've been enslaved.

Angry tears fall from my lashes. "Remove their shackles," I demand to Maloryn and Thalen. "Now."

"The Commander has the key," Maloryn says grimly.

Ronin moves closer. "Stand back," he says.

We all step away, and I watch in awe as he shifts into his draken form immediately. He opens his mouth and releases a stream of flame at the wall where the chains are attached. They melt and fall away. He shifts back into his two-legged form.

I take one of the women's hands as Maloryn stands beside me, scanning them both to check for any other injuries. I hate that they're still bound by their shackles, but we don't have a way to remove them right now. But at least they are free from the wall. "It's all right," I speak softly to the woman with red hair. "We're here to save you."

Maloryn leans over her with his scanner. It beeps, and her eyelids flutter open. She looks up at him, her hazel eyes fixed and unfocused.

He drops his scanner and takes a stumbling half step

back. "It is you," he says in a voice so low I almost miss it. His hands are shaking as he reaches for her, gently cupping her cheek. "You are safe. We will get you out of this place and take you where no one will hurt you. My vow."

Shocked by his tender words and the gentle way he cups her face, I look at him in confusion. He doesn't even like Terrans. Why is he being so nice to her now?

His head snaps to Ronin. "I am coming with you."

"I thought you wanted to stay here," I counter.

"She is my Sy'nan," he murmurs, gesturing to the red-headed woman. "I cannot leave her."

I look at him in shock and then turn to Thalen only to find him staring down at the other woman with a similar look of complete and utter devotion on his face.

A low growl rises in Ronin's throat. "Fine. But when we reach my people, you must do as I say if you want to live. If you do not, they will probably kill you on sight."

Maloryn nods. "Fine. Let us go. Quickly. Before we're discovered."

CHAPTER 30

RONIN

The females are dressed in clothing so thin, they will surely freeze once we go outside. My Ashaya instructs the A'kai to bundle them in thick blankets and furs to keep them warm while we travel.

Thalen insists the Mosauran compound is not far from here, but I will feel better traveling with them, knowing they are at least somewhat protected from the elements.

Terrans are not like my people or the A'kai. They are not able to easily adjust their internal temperature to compensate for extreme weather.

One of the women struggles weakly against Thalen as he gathers her into his arms. They are both still heavily drugged. The smell of their fear thickens the air, and I wrinkle my nose at the acrid scent.

"It's all right," Kyra reassures them. "We are all here to help you. I swear it. We're taking you away from this place."

That seems to settle them a bit.

When I transform into my draken form, the door behind

us opens, and I spin to face it, placing myself protectively in front of my Ashaya and the Terran females.

Fire licks at the back of my throat as I recognize Commander Dural right away. "What do you think you are doing?" he growls. "They are mine!"

I open my mouth and release a wall of fire. He cries out and stumbles backward, out the door and into the snow, writhing on the ground in pain.

Alarms ring throughout the compound as everyone climbs on my back. As soon as they are settled, I speak in Kyra's mind. *"Hold tight to me!"*

She tightens her grip on my neck and I release another stream of flame, melting the metal structure to free us. I flap my wings furiously, climbing up above the compound. I make a low swoop over the outer row of buildings, setting them all aflame as I pass.

Hopefully, the rest of the compound will catch fire. I'd burn it all to ash if I could, but there isn't time as A'kai rush out of the buildings, blasters aimed in our direction.

They fire several volleys our way as I charge into the forest as fast as I can.

The A'kai run faster than most other races, and they follow behind us, firing in our direction, forcing me to dip and weave to avoid taking a direct hit.

Up ahead, I notice a cliff edge and a valley below. If I can reach that, then they will be unable to keep up their pursuit.

I beat my wings furiously, desperate to escape. I failed before and allowed Kyra to be captured. I vow that I will not fail again.

Glancing over my shoulder, I notice several A'kai still behind us. They are as fast as they are lethal, and I cannot let them catch up to us. A blast of light arcs past me, followed quickly by another.

Kyra, Thalen, and Maloryn each return fire with their

own blasters. The edge of the cliff is just up ahead. Once I go beyond it, we will be safe.

As we fly above the forest, I notice something in the far distance. I blink several times as I recognize another Mosauran up ahead.

In draken form with silver gray scales like mine, but green markings on his cheeks and brow. He releases a bellowing roar, and his violet eyes pierce my own.

The scent of Kyra's fear fills the air, but I quickly reassure her as I speak in her mind. *"He is one of my people. He will not harm us."*

"I trust you," she replies, and my heart fills with warmth.

He races toward us, flapping his wings furiously as he picks up speed. Another blast of light rushes past me, and he dips his wing to fly in a wide arc to avoid the hit.

I believe he plans to position himself behind our pursuers. As he passes, I notice someone on his back—a Terran female with long brown hair tied in a braid.

Two puncture wounds on her neck, I recognize as his mark. She is his mate. She must be.

A thunderous roar shakes the air a moment before he breathes out fire, setting a line of trees aflame.

The blasts stop, and he circles back as we drop over the edge of the cliff together, heading straight for the valley and the sea of trees below.

His eyes widen when he notices the two A'kai on my back.

"They're friends," Kyra calls out to him. "They are not the bad guys. I swear."

His Terran companion calls out. "You're Terran?"

"Yes, I'm Kyra."

"I'm Lara," the female replies.

I exchange a glance with the other Mosauran. He motions for me to follow him, but I note his eyes keep returning to

143

the two A'kai males on my back. It is obvious he does not trust them, and I do not blame him. I'd feel the same if our positions were reversed.

He guides us toward a towering mountain in the distance. An ice wall stretches out before it, surrounding the front base like a barrier. A soft glow surrounds it, and I realize it is an energy shield. This is encouraging. They have technology here.

When we reach the wall, the barrier drops, and I follow him to the wall, alighting on top of it. We both shift into two-legged form and regard each other a moment before he steps forward. "I am Commander Markus and this is my mate and Ashaya, Lara."

My eyes widen slightly, surprised by his statement. A Terran is his fated one as well. "I am Commander Ronin and this is my mate and Ashaya, Kyra."

The two A'kai hang back behind me.

Markus looks around me, narrowing his eyes at them. They are both holding the bundled Terran females in their arms. "What are they—"

He stops, and his jaw drops when he notices the shock of blond hair that peeks over the fur.

"They are Healers," I explain. "They helped free us and the Terran women being held at the A'kai compound."

"They need help." Kyra gestures to the women. "They've been drugged."

Another Mosauran lands on the wall, eyeing the A'kai warily. With white scales, purple accents on his cheeks and brow, and green eyes, his gaze travels over Thalen and Maloryn and he growls low in his throat. "Release the Terrans," he grinds out. "Now."

"Stand down, Rokan," Markus commands. "This is Commander Ronin." He gestures to me. "He has vouched for them."

Rokan's gaze shifts to a Terran female near the base of the mountain with short, reddish-brown hair. Her brown eyes are wide as she stares at the two A'kai, and the scent of her fear is so thick I can smell it all the way up here. Rokan flies down to her and takes her hand. "It is all right, Emma," I hear him speak softly. "You are safe."

"Are you sure we can trust them?" she asks, and I know she is not speaking of me and the Terrans, but of the two A'kai.

"I will not let anyone hurt you," he vows. "Ever."

She nods shakily.

He regards her so tenderly, I wonder if they are mated as well.

Another Terran female with long blond hair comes up beside her. Her brow furrows as she glances at us, but Lara—Commander Markus's mate—waves at her. She guides the scared female back into the mountain.

"Come," Markus says. "We must take the females to the Healers."

"We are both Healers," Thalen says, stepping forward. "I—"

"You will both be escorted until I am satisfied you are not a threat to our mates," Markus states firmly. He motions to Rokan and another Mosauran to watch over them. "I suggest you do not make any sudden moves."

Maloryn glares at Markus. "Are we to be imprisoned?"

"That remains to be seen," Markus replies darkly.

He gestures to another two Mosaurans. "Take the Terrans to the Healers. Now."

Maloryn growls menacingly, his eyes turning black as a feral snarl twists his mouth. He holds the Terran to his chest, refusing to hand her over to the Mosauran. "She is mine," he grinds out. "You *will not* take her from me."

The Mosauran narrows his eyes. "Give her to me or—"

"She is my Sy'nan—my Fated one," he growls. "I will not hand her over to you, Mosauran."

"Yes, you will," Markus thunders. "If you do not, I will have you both imprisoned."

Maloryn's nostrils flare, and he glances at Thalen. Thalen dips his chin in a subtle nod, and they both hand the Terran females over to the Mosaurans."

"We are going with you," Thalen states firmly.

One of the Mosaurans nods. "Follow me."

I watch as they leave, heading into the mountain.

CHAPTER 31

RONIN

Kyra rushes to Lara and they embrace warmly, each of them shedding tears of joy. "It's so nice to see another Terran," Kyra whispers.

My mate appears overjoyed to be reunited with one of her people. I notice several other Terran females rushing out of the mountain to walk toward her and Lara.

One of them is followed by a V'loryn and the other by a Lycaon. Panic fills me at the site of the Lycaon. I grasp Kyra's arm and pull her behind me, spreading my wings wide to shield her as my claws extend. I level an icy glare at him. "Do not come any closer, Lycaon."

"It's all right," Markus says quickly. "This is Luken. He lives here with us. He is mated to a Terran as well. This is his mate—Elain." He gestures to a female beside him with long, red hair and golden-brown eyes.

My gaze travels over the Lycaon warrior. His glowing orange eyes study me with a piercing gaze as he tips up his chin. "I am Luken. Alpha of this pack." He gestures to everyone around him. "I—"

"How many times must we go over this," a V'loryn male with short, dark hair and glowing green eyes says as he comes up behind him. He arches a brow. "You are not our Alpha."

Luken crosses his arms over his chest. "You agreed to become part of this pack, Vorek," he states firmly. "And I *am* the Alpha."

Vorek huffs out a frustrated sigh. I watch in shock as a Terran female with long blond hair moves to his side. He wraps a possessive arm around her waist. She smiles up at him, and his expression softens as she speaks. "You know he's only teasing you, my love."

He arches a brow, and I'm shocked when I notice a hint of a smile curving his mouth. V'loryns are known to never show emotion, so this is completely unexpected. "So you say," he replies, and she laughs softly.

I stare at them all in shock. "You all live here... together?" I ask.

Markus nods.

This is completely unheard of. While the Mosauran Empire does have an alliance with the Aerilon, and an uneasy truce with the V'loryns, we are not exactly on friendly terms. And the Lycaons we do not deal with at all, if we can help it.

Markus turns to me. "Where did you come from? How did you find us?"

"We got pulled into a wormhole and had to use an escape pod to land several days ago. We detected your distress signal as we came down and have been searching for it ever since. How long have you been here?"

"We have been stranded here for the past five cycles," Markus says, and I realize he was here long before we even formed the alliance with the Aerilon—our former sworn enemies.

He gestures to the mountain behind him. "We have claimed this territory and made our home here. You are welcome to stay with us."

My heart sinks. "Is there no escape from this world then?" I glance at my mate, upset that I cannot offer her a better life than one stranded on a desolate ice planet.

"Not yet," Markus says. "But we have not given up hope."

CHAPTER 32

KYRA

I'm so happy to find more Terrans. As Markus speaks to Ronin, Lara fills me in on how they met.

Something moves in the corner of my eye, and I turn to see something flying toward us. I gasp when I realize it's an Aerilon carrying a Terran woman. His skin is light purple, and his wings are like a dragonfly's but much larger. He looks just like what I imagine a Fae prince in a fairy tale would look like.

Ronin wraps a possessive arm around my waist, narrowing his eyes. "An Aerilon approaches."

I don't understand his reaction. I thought he said the Aerilon were good guys.

Markus puts a hand on his shoulder. "That is Al'iro and his mate, Violet. He is a friend."

Ronin relaxes. "He is mated to a Terran as well?"

Markus smiles. "Come, there is much to discuss. We have formed an alliance with the V'loryns, Aerilon, and Lycaons." His expression turns grave. "Did you see any other Terrans with the A'kai? We have been searching for them. We have rescued many from the A'kai that landed here not long ago."

Ronin wraps his arm and wing protectively around me. "No, we did not see any others. How many A'kai are there on this world?"

"Many," Markus replies grimly.

His eyes dart to me before returning to Ronin. "Do not worry. We formed the alliance with the others to protect the Terrans and to rescue the ones that are still being held. Your mate will be safe here with us."

Lara takes my hand and smiles warmly. "You'll like it here, Kyra. Everyone is so nice and so friendly. It's like one big family."

I offer a smile in return. Even if we're stuck here, I know, from experience, there are much worse places to be.

We follow her and another woman named Alana into the mountain. Alana is married to the V'loryn guy—Vorek. He walks beside her, one arm looped around her waist.

The air in here is surprisingly crisp instead of earthy and damp like I'd expected. It's also not dark or cramped like I worried it might be.

Several lights are spaced out evenly along each tunnel. The light reflects softly off the smooth slate gray and black stone walls that are carved into perfect angles. Whatever tools they used to hollow out these passages was so precise that there are no sharp edges and the entire space is large enough for five people to walk side-by-side. The ceilings are tall as well, so it doesn't feel closed in.

There are several larger caverns where the various tunnels intersect, and I try to memorize all the turns we take as we make our way through the mountain.

When we reach the Med Center, I'm surprised when Lara and Alana explain that this area is actually part of the Mosauran ship that crashed and embedded itself into the mountain. The Med Center is completely intact. A viewscreen looks out onto the wall and the forest beyond.

All the power for the mountain runs out from this vessel. There are five medical beds and the entire space is pristine polished metal and glass with several monitors and cabinets full of supplies and medicines.

I notice the other two women lying on medical beds while a Mosauran stands over them, studying the readout of his scanner. He has dark gray scales and piercing silver eyes. Lara points to him. "That's Healer Siran."

He turns to face us. "Do you know their names?"

"No. They were unconscious when we found them."

Thalen and Maloryn stand off to the side, each of them glaring at the Mosaurans with murderous rage.

"Thalen? Maloryn?" a voice calls out and everyone stills.

My jaw drops when I notice another A'kai walking toward us. He has short, black hair and glowing green eyes. I'm shocked to see him holding hands with a Terran woman.

He rushes to Thalen. "Erolas?" Thalen smiles at him, and then turns his attention to the woman. "I was afraid you were both dead."

She smiles. "I never got to thank you for saving us, Thalen. It is lovely to finally be able to see you."

My brow furrows. Lara leans in and whispers, gesturing to the woman. "Mina temporarily lost her sight when she was first captured by the A'kai. It wasn't until they found us that Healer Siran was able to restore her sight."

My jaw drops.

Markus steps forward and addresses Erolas. "This is your friend that you have been searching for?"

"Yes," Erolas replies. He looks at Maloryn and claps a hand on his shoulder as well. "They are both good men, Commander."

CHAPTER 33

RONIN

'm shocked that Commander Markus not only had an A'kai already living among them, but that he addresses this one as his equal. He must greatly respect Erolas.

"You will understand if I have them observed and under guard for a few days," Markus says, and I recognize the question in his statement.

Erolas nods. "I do, Markus." His gaze shifts to his A'kai friends. "You will see that they are honorable men."

The V'loryn—Vorek—steps forward, arching a condescending brow. "Is that wise, Markus? Perhaps we should lock them up and question them first."

Erolas gives him an incredulous look. "These are my friends. They will not hurt anyone."

Vorek's glowing green eyes shift to them, narrowing. "If you dare try to harm my mate, I will not hesitate to end you both."

Markus steps between them. He turns to Vorek. "They helped the others to escape."

155

"Why would you do this?" Vorek asks them.

Thalen steps forward, gesturing to the blond women, lying on the medical bed. "Because she is my Sy'nan. And the other is his."

Maloryn studies Vorek warily as Vorek's mouth drifts open, but he quickly snaps it shut as his mate—Alana—moves to his side. "They have Terran mates, my love. They're like Erolas. They won't hurt us."

He cups her cheek and gives her a tender look. "You know I only worry for your safety, my Alana." He places his palm over her lower abdomen. "Both of you."

I blink several times. "She carries your fledgling?"

Vorek's head snaps to me and a hint of irritation shifts into his gaze. "My *child*," he corrects. "Yes."

Alana turns to Kyra. "It seems Terran biology is highly adaptable. From what we've gathered through medical scans, it seems that we're able to procreate naturally with every race we've come across so far: Mosauran, V'loryn, Aerilon, Lycaon, and A'kai."

Thalen looks at Erolas. "This is true?"

He nods and loops his arm around his Terran mate—Mina. "She already carries our child."

Thalen blinks several times and Maloryn's eyes travel over his Sy'nan. It seems this news is a shock to them both.

When Healer Siran insists upon assessing Kyra, she lies down on a med table and allows him to move the scanner over her, along with the ion wand to cleanse her.

"She is a bit malnourished, but healthy otherwise," he reports. His brow furrows deeply as he studies the rest of the readout. "There are several healed bone fractures visible. When did—"

"The Masters used to beat us," Kyra says, answering his unspoken question.

I move to her side and take her hand. She lifts her gaze to

me with tears in her eyes. I gently brush a stray tendril of hair back from her face, tucking it behind her ear. "You are safe here now, my Ashaya. I will allow no one to harm you ever again."

Even as these words leave my mouth, I am ashamed. I should have protected her better. Instead, I got us caught. I failed her and she would probably be dead if not for the help we received from Thalen and Maloryn. As much as I despise the A'kai, we would not have made it without them.

As I study Kyra, it occurs to me that she may no longer desire me as her mate. If she were a Mosauran female, she would reject me now for having failed to protect her. I would be considered an unworthy suitor for this failure.

My heart is heavy, but I force myself to push down my sadness. We are among my people, and she is safe now. That is all that matters.

I observe as she speaks with the Mosauran—Rokan. Perhaps she is already considering someone else for a mate, instead of me. I curl my hands into fists at my sides, angry at myself for my failures.

Rokan laughs at something she says, and I observe in devastation as she laughs heartily in return.

Healer Siran gestures to the two women that we rescued who are lying on the med beds. "I must place them in Med Repair Units." His eyes shift to Thalen and Maloryn. "It will be many hours before they awaken."

They exchange a glance and then turn back to Healer Siran. "We wish to remain here, then."

"Of course," he says.

I pull him aside and whisper in his ear. "I need something to suppress my mating cycle."

His gaze sweeps to Kyra, and he nods in understanding. "I will speak with her about contraception as well."

"Thank you, but that will probably not be necessary."

He frowns. "Why not?"

"I failed her," I admit. "We were caught by the A'kai."

Markus walks up to us. "I could not help but overhear you, brother," he says. "But I believe you should know something."

"What is it?"

"Terran females are not like Mosaurans," he explains. "She will not reject you because of this."

Hope fills me. "How do you know?"

His gaze sweeps to his own Terran mate, across the room. "I have experience with these things."

I pray he is right.

Siran runs the ion cleansing wand over me before he gives me my injection. It is good to have the stench of the A'kai cleansed from my scales.

I observe as he injects Kyra with a contraceptive agent. She smiles at me. "That didn't hurt at all."

"I am glad." What I do not tell her is that I can barely feel the effects of the suppressant. My need for her is so strong, I fear I've waited too long, and it will not work. I will have to speak with her about staying in separate rooms.

I do not want to pressure her into mating. She may not be ready, and I do not want to push my needs onto her, especially if she has decided she no longer wants me.

CHAPTER 34

KYRA

It's late and I'm so tired when Lara and Markus offer to take us to our rooms. "You have spare quarters?" I ask, surprised by how large this complex is here inside the mountain.

Markus turns to me. "We've been expanding this place in the hopes of finding more Terrans and taking them in."

"I'll be so glad to get some sleep," I murmur, leaning against Ronin. "I'm so tired I can barely keep my eyes open."

They guide us down a long hallway lined with metal doors. "How did you do all of this?" I ask.

"We've been scavenging parts from other wrecked ships, including technology." Lara gestures to the lights lining the corridor. "The power cells from the wrecked Mosauran ship and the ones we brought from the V'loryn and Lycaon ships have been linked together to provide us with power for the entire complex, including the energy barrier shield that surrounds the mountain."

"We found an abandoned Craven ship on our journey here," Ronin says. "The power cells were still working on that vessel. Perhaps we can scavenge parts from it as well."

"What of the Craven?" Markus asks. "Did you find any sign of them?"

Ronin shakes his head. "I believe they are dead. No one had been there in a long time."

"There are others here," Markus says grimly. "Luken found a wrecked Tauro ship and evidence that perhaps one of them may have survived."

"Are the Tauro bad?" I ask.

"Our people do not have many dealings with them," Ronin replies. "They are mostly corsairs and mercenaries. As a result, they usually try to avoid the sovereign space of our Empire."

Tauro, Craven, A'kai, Mosaurans, Lycaons, V'loryns, Aerilon… I run through the various species, wondering how many others might be stranded on this world. A small shiver runs down my spine as I think of all the A'kai potentially roaming this planet.

As if sensing this, Ronin wraps an arm around my waist and pulls me into his side. He presses a tender kiss to the top of my head. "We are safe here," he murmurs.

Just that tender amount of affection makes my heart melt. He's perfect and I'm so glad we found this place. Even if we can't leave this planet, at least we've found somewhere to make a home.

We stop in front of a door, and Markus has us press our palms to the panel beside it, coding it to recognize us for entrance.

My eyes go wide as we step through the threshold. A large bed sits against the far wall, piled high with white furs. There's a sofa along another wall, and in an adjoining room, there is a cleansing room. A sunken pool sits in the center of the floor.

A light mist of steam rises from the surface of the water. I open my mouth to ask about this, but Markus interrupts. "This entire mountain complex has a warm spring that runs through it. Our engineers have managed to direct and channel it to the various rooms for plumbing and such."

He explains the various other technologies, like lights and the rest of the plumbing they've incorporated. I can't help but stare at everything in awe. I'd thought we would have to rough it on this world, but it seems like we'll be living in comfort.

Markus gestures to a display near the door. "This is the comm system. You press this,"—he points to the upper left-hand corner of the screen—"if you need to contact someone."

"Commander Markus!" A voice comes through the speaker. "There is A'kai activity just outside the perimeter!"

Fear tightens my chest.

Ronin looks at Markus and nods. "Let's go."

Markus turns to Lara. "Remain here. We will investigate and return as soon as possible."

Ronin slips his arms around me, wrapping me up in his wings.

"I'm going with you," I state firmly.

He cups my chin and tips my face up to his, sealing his mouth over mine in a tender kiss. "Not this time," he says. "You are tired. You—"

"I'm not tired," I protest.

His expression softens. "I can see it in your eyes, my Ashaya. I will return to you soon."

Ronin presses another kiss to my lips and then turns and rushes out the door with Markus.

Lara sighs heavily. "It's their instinct, I think," she muses. "They are very protective of their mates." She drops a hand

JESSICA GRAYSON & ARIA WINTER

to her stomach. "He's been especially protective since we found out I'm expecting."

I gaze at her abdomen. "Ronin told me it was possible. So we've been careful."

Her brow furrows. "How did he know?"

"Their people have been rescuing ours from slavers," I explain. "Apparently, their crown prince is married to a Terran woman."

Hope lights her face. "Do they know where Terra is?"

I shake my head. "They have been searching, but they haven't found it yet."

"I'm glad someone is searching for them," she says. "It was awful being held for so long. Some of us are still—" She stops short, swallowing hard as tears brighten her eyes. "Emma is so traumatized she barely speaks. Rokan is her constant shadow."

I think back on Rokan, with his white scales, green eyes and the purple highlights on his cheeks and brow. I remember him comforting a Terran woman when we first arrived and she was upset at the sight of Thalen and Maloryn.

She continues. "He is so protective of her; he hardly ever leaves Emma's side."

"Are they... together?" I ask, curious to know.

"No." A faint smile tilts her lips. "But if it were to happen, I certainly wouldn't be surprised. Neither would anyone else here, I think."

She walks to the cleansing room and comes back out with some folded clothing. She hands it to me. "Here. You can wear this until we make something a bit more tailored for you specifically."

It's similar to what I already have on. A large tunic, loose fitting pants, and a fur cloak to wear for extra warmth.

She glances at the door. "I'm going outside to see what's happening. Do you want to come with me?"

"They asked us to stay here."

She pats the blaster at her hip. "I know, but I'd feel better being out there in case they need us."

I like Lara, and I think we're going to get along well. I pull the blaster from my belt as I smile at her. "Me too."

CHAPTER 35

RONIN

As we stand on the wall, Commander Dural of the A'kai glares up at us from below. I notice the left side of his face is now ruined; his green skin appearing melted from my fire. His people heal quickly, like mine do, but without his Healers, he cannot regenerate his flesh properly.

Five of his warriors stand behind him, each of them with a Terran female.

Their wrists are bound behind their backs, and they have slave collars around their necks.

"Look what we found while in pursuit of you, Commander Ronin," Dural says tauntingly.

"Why are you here?" I growl.

"Turn yourself over to me, along with the A'kai traitors within your walls"—his eyes narrow at Thalen, Erolas, and Maloryn—"and I will give the Terran females to your people."

Commander Markus steps forward. "You will give them

to us, but you will receive nothing in return but the opportunity to leave here alive, Dural."

Dural arches a brow. "I thought your honor would demand that you pay any price in order to save females, Markus. Will you really refuse to give three A'kai traitors and one Mosauran to me?"

One of the Terran females whimpers as the A'kai holding her tugs on the chain attached to her collar. Dural spins and backhands her across the cheek, causing her to stumble and fall.

He turns back to us, and a sinister smile curves his mouth. "Well, what shall it be? Will you accept my offer?"

Markus narrows his eyes. "I understand why you want the A'kai, but why do you want Ronin?"

He asks this to buy time while Luken and Vorek make their way downwind and behind the A'kai with a few of their men.

Dural does not know this, but he will not leave here alive today.

"He ruined my face, and I will make him pay for it," Dural replies darkly. "Now, hand him over, as well as the A'kai traitors in your midst."

Drawing in a steadying breath, I turn to Markus. I have to be convincing for this to work. We knew Dural would have demands and we agreed to do whatever it took to stall for time to surround his men.

I doubt he wants me only to have his revenge. I suspect he kept me alive, in the first place, because he wanted a Mosauran to try to breach this complex.

"Commander Markus." I turn to him, trying my best to appear defeated. "I will sacrifice myself to save the Terran females. Please watch over my Ashaya."

Markus clenches his jaw. "There must be another way."

"No," Dural practically seethes. "There is not. Now, give them to me," he demands. "Or I will kill the Terran females."

Three Mosaurans grab Thalen, Erolas, and Maloryn, pretending they are going to force them to go as well.

The A'kai each growl low and menacingly, trying to be as convincing as possible. It seems all four of us are rather convincing actors, because Dural's lips curl up in a sinister grin. He thinks he has won.

Markus gives me a reluctant nod. "Very well." He turns back to Dural. "Now, give us the females."

"First, give me the Mosauran and the A'kai," Dural counters.

"No," Markus states firmly. "We will make the exchange at the same time."

Dural nods. "Fine."

"Lower the shield," Markus commands.

CHAPTER 36

KYRA

Lara and I are quiet as we make our way to the wall. We ascend a spiraling staircase up one of the ice towers, careful to remain out of sight. When we reach the top, we find Alana already there with another woman. I recognize her as the one married to the Lycaon. I think her name is Elain.

"What are you doing here?" Lara hisses under her breath.

"I could ask you the same thing," Alana counters. She pulls the blaster from her belt. "Vorek is out there with Luken."

"Yeah," Elain says. "I hate when Luken does stuff like this. He thinks he's invincible. I told him to stay behind the wall, but he and Vorek came up with this plan and now—"

An electric hum fills the air, and we watch as the shield goes down.

Chaos erupts as the A'kai begin firing their blasters toward the wall and to Ronin and the rest of the warriors.

Several other A'kai rush out from the forest, charging forward as they begin shooting as well.

Ronin and Markus shift in an instant, flying off the wall and toward the A'kai, barely managing to dodge the several blasts of light arcing toward them.

The other Terrans and I begin firing from our position. I hit one of the A'kai, and he drops like a stone to the ground.

Vorek and Luken race out of the forest, surrounding the A'kai with more V'loryns and Lycaons.

The V'loryns are just as terrifying as Thalen, Erolas, and Maloryn. Their eyes are black and their fangs and claws are extended as they tear into the A'kai.

The Lycaons look like wolves, but so much bigger than any I've ever seen as they clash with the A'kai in a fury of claws and fangs.

I take down two more A'kai. One of them manages to get back up, but Ronin sets him on fire, burning him to ash in an instant.

After what feels like forever, it's over. The A'kai are all dead, including Commander Dural. The Terran women are obviously shaken and terrified as Ronin and the others walk toward them.

Lara calls out to them. "It's all right. You are safe now. No one here will harm you."

Their eyes snap to the A'kai. Thalen, Erolas, and Maloryn stand back, giving them space. After being held by the A'kai, I doubt they're going to want to have anything to do with those three, despite that they are on our side.

Ronin rushes over to me, and I let out a surprised squeak as he gathers me in his arms. His expression is thunderous as he storms back into the mountain without saying a word.

"What are you doing?"

"I asked you to stay inside where it was safe, but you did not listen."

"We looked out for each other when we were traveling to get here. How is this any different?"

He clenches his jaw. "Because now we have a nest where you do not have to risk your life anymore. The other warriors and I will—"

"I'm not helpless, Ronin."

We step inside our quarters, and he carefully places me on my feet.

"Ronin, I—"

He shakes his head. "Forgive me. My mating heat has been triggered by your scent. You are at your fertile peak and because I have not yet claimed you, my protective instincts are heightened." He grits his teeth. "You could have been hurt, Kyra. I failed to protect you before, and I will not fail you again."

"You didn't fail me," I protest.

"Yes, I did. And if you were a Mosauran female, you would reject me for this weakness."

"But I'm not Mosauran, Ronin." I stretch up on my toes and press a tender kiss to his lips. "You've kept me safe from the moment we met. And all you have done is to love and care for me since then."

"You still want me?" His brow furrows deeply. "Even though I failed you?"

"Of course, I still want you. You didn't fail me. I lo—"

He captures my mouth in a claiming kiss as he presses my back to the wall. He lifts me up, bracing me against it, and I wrap my legs around his hips. His stav presses insistently against my core. I cup his cheek, and his golden eyes meet mine in a smoldering gaze. "What do you need?"

"I need to leave," he rasps.

I inhale sharply at the stab of hurt from his words. "Why?"

Perhaps he doesn't want me after all. Maybe he's the one who changed his mind.

"Healer Siran gave me a suppressant for my mating heat, but it is not working," he grinds out. "Creator, help me, but I want you so much I can hardly stand it." He clenches his jaw as his gaze holds mine. "I do not want to pressure you into a mating."

Relief fills me. It's not that he doesn't want me. It's that he wants me so much he's afraid of pressuring me. What he doesn't realize is that I want him too.

I twine my arms around his neck and press my lips to his in a tender kiss. He groans as I flick my tongue against his lips, asking for entrance. "Kyra, please," he murmurs into my mouth. "I am weak right now. I must leave."

I pull back just enough to study him. "What if I want you, too?"

He cups my chin. His pupils are blown wide so that only a thin rim of gold is barely visible around the edges. "You are sure?"

I remember what he told me of the mating battle. I'm not sure what he expects, but I want to make sure that there is no doubt in his mind that I desire him. "Shav-rhokan," I state firmly, staring deep into his eyes.

He stills and then drops his chin to stare across at me through heavy brows. His gaze is both predatory and filled with desire, every muscle tense as if it is taking everything inside him to hold on to his control. "You are absolutely certain?" He growls low in arousal, and I love that he asks again. He is a good man, and I know how much he loves me.

My entire body hums in awareness of him as my heart pounds in my chest. "Yes."

He leans in and a short puff of air skims across my neck as he scents me. A low rumbling growl vibrates deep in his chest, sending small ripples of pleasure straight to my core.

My heart beats wildly in my chest as he wraps his wings around me, drawing me even closer.

I'm breathless with anticipation. There is no space between us. His body is pressed solidly against mine as he dips his head and lightly skims the tip of his nose along my temple, down to my jaw and to the curve of my neck and shoulder again.

My heart races, and every nerve ending is on fire at his touch. He reaches between us and slices away my clothing, careful not to nick me with his sharp claws.

His golden eyes search mine, full of desire. "I could have just removed those, you know," I gently tease. "You didn't have to ruin them."

He growls as his stav presses against me, and I moan at the sensation. "I could not wait," he rasps. "I need you now."

He cups one breast, and I gasp as he brushes the pad of his thumb across the sensitive peak.

His warm breath whispers across my skin as he opens his mouth just above the curve of my shoulder.

Something sharp touches my sensitive flesh, and I try to twist, putting up a mock form of the struggle he would expect if I were a Mosauran female as we were locked in the mating battle.

He goes still. "Have I hurt you?" he speaks softly, his voice full of panic.

I cup his cheek, guiding his lips to mine in a tender kiss before I whisper. "No. I want you. Don't stop, Ronin."

His eyes dilate once more and his lips pull back to expose sharp fangs. His hands possessively trace over my form, claiming my body as his as he bears me to the floor.

He lowers his head, and I feel the slight sting of his sharp fangs against my skin as he leaves a light mark of claiming on my flesh.

A low moan escapes me as he cups my mons possessively. His touch is fire, and I want more.

"You are mine," his voice whispers in my mind. Desire pools deep inside me as he wraps his wings around me and breathes into my ear. "Tell me you are mine."

"Yours," I barely manage.

I trace my fingers down his powerful form, feeling every delicious dip and curve of muscle beneath his scales as I move from his chest to his abdomen. When I reach his stav, he hisses as I wrap my hand around his length and guide his tip to my entrance.

He's so large my fingers cannot entirely encircle him. His stav is covered with a line of thick ridges and my thighs involuntarily squeeze together as I imagine what he will feel like inside me.

He groans as I part my thighs even more to accept him. "I want you," I breathe against his lips. "I love you, Ronin."

His gaze is full of fire and hunger as the hard planes of muscle ripple beneath the surface as his chest rises and falls with ragged breaths. His nostrils flare. "I can scent your need, my Ashaya," he growls. "I will take you many times this night."

I'm breathless with anticipation as he wraps his wings around me. His gaze holds mine and a soft moan escapes my lips as he slowly enters me. My head falls back as I accept him into my body, relishing the deep stretch in my channel as he fills me completely.

He groans as he sheathes himself fully inside me. "So tight," he rasps.

A slight pinch of pain, as he breaks through my barrier, quickly turns into pleasure as he begins to move deep inside me.

The delicious friction of his stav deep in my channel is exquisite as overwhelming sensation moves through me. It's too much and not enough all at once. He seals his mouth over mine in a branding kiss.

"Mine," he growls.

I trace my hands over his back, feeling the powerful muscles of his body as he pumps into me. Each stroke becoming more forceful and deeper.

He growls again, and the vibrations move straight through me. My toes curl with pleasure as he quickens his pace. "You are mine," he breathes into my mouth. "And I am yours."

My head falls back. I'm so close to the edge.

He grips my chin and tips my face back to his. "I want to watch you as you find your release."

His gaze holds mine, full of fire and possession as he thrusts into me. My body tightens around him a moment before I fall over the edge, crying out his name as wave after wave of pleasure moves through me.

My release triggers his own. His stav begins to pulse in my core as he erupts deep inside me, filling me with the delicious warmth of his seed. It feels as if it goes on forever, and another orgasm sweeps through me, this one even stronger than the last.

With our bodies still joined, he pulls away just enough to meet my gaze evenly. A softly glowing light centers on his chest and begins to grow even brighter.

"What is that?" I ask.

"My lifeforce. I must use it to seal you to me, my Ashaya. Do you accept?"

I love him and I want him. I trust him completely. "What does it mean?"

"It will seal our bond. You would be mine forever."

Tears fill my eyes, and my heart is so full I can't speak.

A gorgeous smile lights his face, and he nuzzles my head. "I want no one but you, my Ashaya. You are my heart."

I press my lips to his and then whisper against them. "I accept."

He places his palm directly over the glowing spot, and when he pierces his chest with his claws, the light begins to pulse. Extending his hand to my chest, directly over my heart, the tips of his claws lightly pierce my skin.

A small hiss of pain escapes my lips at the sharp sting, but it only lasts a moment before it is gone.

He lowers himself so that his chest presses against mine. Heat sears my skin and he swallows my gasp with a claiming kiss.

Intense warmth blooms from the site and across my entire body. I close my eyes as delicious heat flows through me in a wave of pure and utter bliss.

When I open my eyes, I'm struck by the sudden awareness of our hearts in sync, beating in time as one. "You are my heart, Kyra," he whispers. "And I am yours."

He's still buried deep inside me, and I gasp as he begins stroking into me. "I want you again," he murmurs against my lips. "Will you accept me?"

I tighten my arms and legs around him as he kisses me long and deep. "Yes," I barely manage.

He stares down at me, his gaze full of fire and possession. "I will take you many times this night, my Ashaya, if you will have me."

"I'm yours," I whisper.

He changes the angle of his hips, sinking impossibly deeper in my core and a low moan escapes my mouth as his stav begins to pulse inside me once again.

EPILOGUE

KYRA

It's only been a few weeks, but this mountain already feels like home to me. I slip on my robe to get ready for bed when warm arms wrap around me from behind, pulling me into the solid warmth of Ronin's chest. He leans down and gently nuzzles my neck before pressing a tender kiss to my temple.

"I missed you this day," he whispers in my ear.

I smile. "You were only gone a few hours guarding the wall, my love."

He stands and curls his wings around me. "Any time away from you is too long."

Lifting me into his arms, he carries me to the bed. He moves over me, pressing a line of tender kisses down the length of my body.

He stills when he reaches my abdomen, and I lift my head. "What is it?"

"Your scent has changed," he murmurs. He splays his palm

over my lower abdomen. "I believe you may be carrying our fledgling."

My head jerks back. "Are you sure? It's only been a few weeks since we first made love and I—"

"Yes," he replies without hesitation. "I am certain."

"But Healer Siran gave me a contraceptive injection," I counter, trying to temper my hope. I know we've only been together a short while, but the idea of a family with Ronin is wonderful. I've already been regretting the contraceptive injection. Especially after I found out it can last six months to a year.

If I've learned anything since I was taken, it's that life is short and I want to grab all the happiness I can while I'm able.

His expression falls. "If you do not wish to carry our child, I am sure that Healer Siran will—"

I press a finger to his lips to silence him. "It's not that," I say quickly. "I just… don't want to get my hopes up and then find out that we're wrong. That's all."

His golden eyes search mine. "You want our fledgling?"

"I love you." I cup his cheek. "I want a family with you, Ronin."

His lips curve up in a devastatingly handsome smile. "Do you want to go to the Healer? He will confirm that you carry our child in your womb."

"You're that sure about it?"

Lifting me into his arms, he carries me out of our room, down the corridor and straight to the Med Center. Healer Siran frowns when we enter. "Is everything all right?"

"I believe my Ashaya is with child," Ronin states proudly. "But we wish for you to confirm this."

Healer Siran blinks several times. "But I gave you the contraceptive injection. It should have worked."

Ronin sets me down on the exam table, and Siran runs

the scanner over me. His eyes widen, and he gives me an apologetic look. "I—I do not understand what happened. I thought it would work, but—"

"I'm pregnant, then?" I ask, excitement building in my chest.

He gives me a grim nod.

I pull him into a hug. "Thank you!"

When I let him go, he studies me in confusion. "You are not upset?"

"No. I'm happy," I tell him, observing as his expression turns into one of relief. "Well, you will be glad to know that the fledgling is healthy, according to my scans."

Ronin lifts me up, pressing his lips to mine as he wraps his wings solidly around me. "I love you," I whisper.

"Of course, you do." He flashes a handsome and teasing smile. "I am perfect, remember?" He places has hand on my abdomen. "And our fledgling will be perfect as well, my Ashaya."

I laugh softly. I place my hand over his, on my belly, as I blink back tears. "You *are* perfect, my love. My strong, hand-some, perfect, Mosauran warrior."

His golden eyes stare deep into my own as he drops his forehead gently to mine. "Yours," he breathes. "Always."